Julian didn't expect to have a second chance at life. Then his son dragged him out of the forest, and he met Kaspar.

Kaspar thought he'd eventually go home now that the carriers in the forest are free, but Julian walked into his life and made him rethink everything.

Julian and Kaspar want to be together, but even with the new laws and the majority of the council on their side, it doesn't mean that people will look kindly at two carriers who want to be together, even if one of them thinks he can't have any more children.

That's only one of their problems. Kaspar is much younger than Julian, who already has an adult son. Julian doesn't know how to live with people after spending the past twenty-five years in the forest.

And the humans are coming, something that could cause more problems than anything they are prepared for.

In Spite of Everything
Copyright © 2020 Catherine Lievens
ISBN: 978-1-4874-2868-6
Cover art by Angela Waters

Published by eXtasy Books Inc or
Devine Destinies, an imprint of eXtasy Books Inc

Look for us online at:
www.eXtasybooks.com or www.devinedestinies.com

In Spite of Everything
Allegheny Shifters Book 6

By

Catherine Lievens

CHAPTER ONE

"I can't believe you said that!" Chris yelled.

Julian sighed and closed his eyes. He hated that Jacob and Chris were fighting — again.

"What do you want me to say? We already talked about this." Jacob sounded angry, but also weary, as if he couldn't do this anymore. If Julian were in his place, he'd probably feel the same way.

Julian knew why Chris and Jacob were fighting. Everyone did. Even though he'd been the last to arrive at the Bishop House, he'd been informed that Chris would one day become the next bobcat alpha. Jacob, on the other hand, was a badger, and a guard. To make things even more complicated, Chris was a carrier. It meant he could get pregnant by Jacob, something his father was bound to be unhappy with. Chris didn't care about that, though. He was strong-willed, and he knew exactly what he wanted in life.

And he wanted Jacob.

The two of them had been fighting over that ever since things had started to get better for the carriers in the forest. Chris's father would eventually come back to get Chris and his twin brother, Nico. He would take them home, and Chris would be without Jacob. Chris had been trying to convince Jacob to move with him to bobcat territory, but Jacob had said no every time.

Julian didn't blame him.

One would think that since Julian had spent most of his life hiding in the forest, he wouldn't understand human beings.

Some days he still had a hard time. But the Bishop House was perfect for him. He was surrounded by people who were like him—shifters, carriers, men who were more vulnerable than most people in the forest. They shared the house with the guards, too, but all of them were good people, like Jacob.

Chris and Jacob should be free to be together. Julian didn't know if they were in love, but he suspected they were It was obvious from the way they looked at each other. But Chris had big things waiting for him in the future. He would become the bobcat alpha, and he would rule over a wide territory and numerous people. Jacob, on the other hand, was only a guard. There was nothing wrong with that, but traditionally, alpha marriages were arranged. The different shifter groups did that to create alliances and gain allies. That wouldn't happen in this case, because Jacob was only a guard, not part of the badger alpha's family.

Julian didn't think it mattered. As far as Thomas, the badger alpha, was concerned, he already had an alliance with the bobcats. He'd taken in the twin sons of the bobcat alpha when carriers had been hunted, and he hadn't asked for anything in return. He was a good man, and it showed in the way he treated his sons. Two of them were carriers, yet he hadn't sold them out. He'd allowed them to choose who they wanted to marry, and they had. They were both happy now, and Thomas wanted the same for all the cete members. He wouldn't have anything to say if Jacob decided to leave. Hell, he'd probably help him, and he would make sure Jacob had everything he needed to start a new chapter of his life.

But Jacob was resistant. Leaving the cete would mean leaving everything he knew behind to become a future alpha mate. He didn't want that, and Julian didn't blame him. The thought of being in a position of responsibility was terrifying, and Julian was more than happy to hide out in the Bishop House. This was where he belonged anyway. He no longer had a place in his gang. He'd left a long time ago, and even though the alpha had since died, he already knew he couldn't go back, not after everything that had happened.

The cete had become his new family, his and the carriers'. He was happy that he and his son had found a family they hadn't known they could have, but he wished that family would stop yelling.

"Why won't you even try?" Chris cried out, pain tingeing his words.

He and Jacob were fighting in the kitchen, which meant none of the other carriers or the guards could go there. It was almost time for dinner, though, and that made things awkward.

Every fight Chris and Jacob had made things awkward. Julian wished he could do more for them, but he'd tried talking to both, and nothing had changed. He knew he wasn't the only one who'd tried. Everyone in the house wanted to see Chris and Jacob happy, but Julian was starting to wonder if they wouldn't be happier separated rather than together. They might be in love, but sometimes, love wasn't enough. No matter how much people tried or how much they felt, it didn't mean they would succeed.

"I can't come with you," Jacob said. His tone was quieter now, but just as torn.

"Because you don't care about me," Chris snapped.

"Of course I care about you."

"Not enough."

Julian had heard enough. He rose from the couch and strode toward the kitchen, ignoring the alarmed glances he got from a few of the carriers who were waiting for the kitchen to be empty. He stepped into the kitchen, and both Chris and Jacob turned to look at him.

Chris was smaller than Jacob, but he seemed to tower over him. Jacob was sitting at the counter with his face in his hands.

Chris's cheeks were flushed, and his hair looked like he'd raked his hands through it more than once. He was breathing heavily, but he shut his mouth as soon as Julian walked in.

"It's almost time for dinner," Julian said.

Chris shook his head. "And you can't wait?" He turned his attention back to Jacob without waiting for an answer. "This isn't over. We're not done talking."

He stomped out, and Jacob apparently couldn't resist having the last word. "We're not talking about this again, Chris," he yelled after Chris. "It won't change anything."

Julian arched a brow at him, and Jacob shook his head and buried his face in his hands again.

Julian decided to leave him to it and headed for the fridge, wondering what he could put together for everyone. It would have to be something quick, since they didn't have time to cook.

"I'm sorry," Jacob said.

Julian should stay out of it. It would be best for everyone, but especially for himself. He'd already tried, and he hadn't made a difference. He wasn't sure he could ignore the pain in Jacob's voice, though.

"When will he leave?" he asked.

"I don't know. *We* don't know. His father wanted to take him and Nico home when the cete was attacked, but thanks to Kari, he allowed them to stay for a little while longer. It won't last forever, though."

"And he's still trying to convince you to go with him."

"I'm pretty sure everyone here knows that's what's happening. He hasn't been discreet about it."

Julian chuckled and reached for a bag of lettuce. If he added stuff to it like cheese and tomatoes, it would make a nice salad. "He's not even *trying* to be discreet. I'm pretty sure even Thomas heard him, and the Bishop House is a long way from the rest of the cete."

"I don't know what to do anymore," Jacob said with a groan.

"What *can* you do? As far as I can see, there are only two options, and it looks to me like you've already decided."

"What options?"

Julian dumped the lettuce into the sink so he could wash it and turned to look at Jacob. "Either you go with him, or you break up with him and stay here."

Jacob scowled. "Why can't I stay here and still be with him?"

Julian smiled sadly. "Because it's not that easy. Because he's not just a guy. He's a carrier, and a future alpha to boot. He will have a lot of responsibilities, and as the alpha, he cannot have a boyfriend who lives in another shifter group. Besides, if things evolve between the two of you, one of you is going to have to move eventually. Will you ask him to give up his future position to live with you here?"

Jacob pulled on a strand of his short hair. "Why not? Why should I have to be the one to move?"

"I've never said it was fair. But life isn't fair most of the time, Jacob. No one said *you* should move, but you're going to have to make a decision . . . and fast. This can't go on. You're disrupting the peace, and God knows most of the people who live here need it."

Jacob rubbed his face. "I'm sorry. It won't happen again."

Julian smiled at him. They both knew that was a lie, but he didn't point that out.

Kaspar almost collided with Chris outside the kitchen. He managed to step to the side before Chris could mow him over, and he watched Chris as he stomped his way upstairs.

He'd heard the fight. He was pretty sure everyone in the house and even a few people outside had heard it. Fights between Jacob and Chris were almost routine by now, and Kaspar wasn't sure anyone could do anything about them. Things would change once Chris moved back home, but no one knew when that would be, and Kaspar couldn't help but wonder what would happen then.

He looked toward the kitchen, then at the stairs again. Kaspar didn't know where Nico, Chris's brother, was, but it wasn't upstairs. Maybe Chris shouldn't be alone. He might not want to see anyone right now, but Kaspar wanted him to know that he wasn't alone. He had friends who would listen to him if he needed them to. Kaspar wasn't about to take a side because he didn't think anyone was wrong in this situation, but he could support Chris.

He followed Chris upstairs.

Chris's bedroom door was closed, of course, but Kaspar quietly knocked. He was surprised when Chris called for him to enter, then realized Chris had probably thought he was Jacob when Chris's eyes widened and his expression crumbled. He flopped back onto his bed and looked away.

Kaspar stepped in and closed the door behind himself. "I'm sorry if I'm bothering you," he said.

"You're not bothering me. Did you need something?"

Kaspar hesitated. Chris was strong. Everyone knew that, including Chris. But sometimes Chris thought being strong meant he couldn't show vulnerability. He was already fighting against the fact that he was a carrier and that carriers never became alphas. It had never been a law, but carriers had been considered weak until recently. Some people still thought that. The last thing Chris needed was for people to think he was weak because he had emotions.

All of that was bullshit.

"You had a fight with Jacob," Kaspar said.

Chris rolled his eyes. "I'm pretty sure everyone knows about that. We're not exactly quiet when we fight."

"Do you want to talk about it?"

Chris shrugged, and for one moment, he looked like the young man he was. He was younger than Kaspar by six years, way too young to become alpha. Luckily for him, that wouldn't happen anytime soon. It didn't mean he didn't have responsibilities, though.

"My father wants me and Nico to go home," Chris said.

"You already knew that would happen."

"I knew it would happen from the time I got here. That's not the problem."

"Jacob is."

Chris laughed darkly. "He *definitely* is. I never expected to fall in love when I got here. Hell, I thought I would hate it here. I didn't want to leave home. I didn't want to hide, and I thought I was strong enough to face the council and everyone else."

"Hiding doesn't mean you're not strong."

"I know. But I thought I couldn't show people that I was afraid."

Kaspar wasn't sure if Chris had ever shown anyone he was afraid, but he didn't point that out. Chris was talking to him, and that was the important thing. "You didn't expect Jacob."

"I didn't. I thought once the carriers were safe, Nico and I would go home and go back to our lives. That's what my father wants me to do. He wants me to go home so he can continue teaching me how to be the next alpha."

"And that's what you want, too."

Chris bit his lower lip. "I've always known I couldn't stay here forever. I'm not a badger shifter."

"You know Thomas doesn't care about that." If anything, the badger alpha had been collecting shifter species. Two of his sons were married to bear shifters, while another was married to a weasel shifter. That wasn't all. The carriers in the house all belonged to different shifter species who shared the forest with the badgers.

"Can you imagine my father's face if I told him I want to stay?" Chris snorted. "I don't think so. Besides, I always expected to go home. I didn't think I would fall in love with Jacob, though." He raked a hand through his hair. "Or for Jacob to be this stubborn."

"You're stubborn, too," Kaspar pointed out.

Chris smiled at him. "You're right. I am. I know I am. But I don't want to leave him. I know I have to go home. My father won't take no for an answer. He expects me to take my rightful place one day. And to do that, I have to know how to lead the pride. I have to learn what he has to teach me. I just don't understand why Jacob won't come with me."

Kaspar took a risk and sat on the edge of Chris's mattress. "Well, the cete needs him more than ever now."

"Why? The carriers are safe."

"For now, sure. But you know there's a human team coming. They're going to look at all of us, including the cete. I wouldn't be surprised if some of the shifters against us try something with the humans to get rid of Thomas. Besides, not all carriers have a home to go back to. Some of us are staying, and we'll need people to protect us."

"Everyone is safe here, though. The Bishop House is far away from the edge of badger territory. I know Thomas is thinking about lowering the number of guards here. The carriers won't be attacked. We have rights now, and everyone knows it."

"There might be new laws in place, but it doesn't mean everyone is going to follow them. Come on, Chris. You know better than that."

"But it's not fair. Why is the cete more important than me?"

Kaspar knew he had to be very careful about what he said. "This is his home, his family. It's the place where he grew up, and where he thought he would live for the rest of his life."

"And I get that. I do. But can't he see that being the next alpha is more important?"

"Not to him. You said you want him to go with you?"

"Of course I do."

"And he doesn't want to. Why?"

"Because he doesn't want to be the alpha mate. He doesn't want to leave the cete. I should be more important than that, but I'm not."

"So you're going to break up?"

Chris's eyes widened, and he shook his head. "Of course not. I'm sure we can find a compromise."

"Can you, though? Because it looks to me like neither of you is ready to compromise. And the thing is, I understand where both of you are coming from. Being the next alpha is important to you. It's something you've been groomed to be ever since you were born, and something everyone expects from you. You don't want to disappoint your father. That's noble. But I also understand why Jacob doesn't want to go with you. He never expected to be an alpha mate, and it's not an easy role to slip into. Besides, the two of you aren't married, and we both know that your father won't be happy if he ever finds out about your relationship."

"That's exactly why Jacob should come with me now. He could get used to being my husband and his role by my side. My father will see that Jacob is the right man for me once he gets to know him."

Kaspar wasn't sure about that. Alpha Wiley loved his sons, and he wanted them to be treated as more than carriers, but that didn't mean he would want his heir to step out of line. He supported the carriers' laws because he wanted Chris and Nico to be respected, but he still wanted Chris to be his heir, because it was tradition and how things had gone for decades. "Whatever happens, one or both of you will have to give up a lot."

"I can't give up. Being the next alpha is important. And not for me. It's important for the *pride.*"

"You're right. It's important. But is it more important than Jacob? Because that's what it's going to come down to in the end, isn't it? If you can't convince Jacob to go with you, and it doesn't look like you will, you'll have to choose. Either *he* is the most important thing in your life, or being the next alpha is."

"Both things are important."

"And I'm not saying it's wrong that you feel that way. In a perfect world, you would have both. In this world, you can't, Chris. You're going to have to choose, and I doubt you'll like the result." Because either way, he would lose something important to him. Kaspar was glad he wasn't in his place, but right now, with Chris looking so tiny and vulnerable, he kind of wished he were. He wanted to take away Chris's pain, but he couldn't.

The only thing he could do was to be there for Chris, and he didn't know how much that would help.

Julian smiled at Kaspar when he saw him coming down the stairs. "Dinner's ready in the kitchen. It's not much, but I didn't have a lot of time to put something together."

"Did you talk to Jacob?"

Julian blinked. "How did you know?"

"I just had a conversation with Chris."

Julian sighed. "From your expression, I doubt you had better results than I did." He looked around. The entrance and the living room were empty, but he could hear voices coming from the kitchen. Most of the inhabitants of the Bishop House were eating right now, and while he liked most of them, they were noisy. He wasn't used to that, and he didn't know if he ever would be after spending most of his life alone with his son in the forest. "How about I grab you one of the sandwiches I made and some salad, and we hide in the living room? We can talk about Chris and Jacob." Julian would talk about anything if that was what it took for him to be able to spend some time with Kaspar.

Kaspar smiled at Julian and put a hand on his shoulder. He gently steered him toward the living room. "I'll go get dinner. You sit down. You just said you got dinner ready, which means you've been on your feet for far longer than I was. Go get some rest."

Julian could feel his cheeks heating. "I'm not tired. It's just dinner, nothing elaborate." He didn't mind being on his feet. If anything, he wasn't used to sitting down as much as he had recently.

He'd been living in the forest for most of his life, utterly alone but for his son. That meant he was used to getting up with the sun, taking care of the garden, growing vegetables, and doing everything on his own. Here at the Bishop House, though, other people helped, and more importantly, there was running water and electricity. Those things made Julian's life more comfortable, and he was a bit lost. He didn't have as much work as he had before, and he wasn't quite sure what to do with his time now.

"Go on," Kaspar gently pushed.

Julian couldn't help but nod. "Thank you. I'll be in the living room, then." It wasn't the most private setting to have a conversation, but with everyone else eating, it was good enough.

Julian settled onto one of the couches and looked out the window. He wished he could do more for Chris and Jacob. He hoped the two of them would find their way to each other. They deserved to be happy.

"Here you go," Kaspar said as he walked into the living room holding a tray.

It looked as though he'd put quite a bit of effort into making their plates look good, and Julian smiled at him when he accepted his. "Thank you. You really shouldn't have."

"Of course I should. I know you can do this on your own, but you should have someone who takes care of you every so often. Everyone should."

Julian didn't know how to answer that, so he focused on the food.

Kaspar wasn't done, though. He ate a few bites of his sandwich, then asked, "What were you thinking about just now? You look worried."

"I was thinking that Chris and Jacob should be happy. Chris, especially, had to hide such an important part of himself for so long. It's not fair that even though the carriers are free now, he's not."

"We should all be happy. Life is unfair, and as carriers, we've seen our fair share of that—especially you. You deserve to be happy, too. You deserve to have someone in your life, just like Chris and Jacob do."

Julian hadn't expected the conversation to go that way. "I *am* happy."

"Well, of course you are. You have your son, and he's a great guy."

"I'm also living here now. I didn't mind living in the forest. I was used to it. But trust me, there's something good to be said about being able to take a warm shower anytime I want one."

Kaspar chuckled. "I can see that. But what about your personal life? Your love life? Don't you think you deserve someone?"

Julian bit his lower lip and forced himself to look away from Kaspar. "I spent my life alone. I'm too old for anything different, and that's okay." Julian knew the chances that he'd meet someone who could accept what he was and what he'd gone through were slim. But he had Kari, and in the near future, he would have Kari's baby. He would be a grandfather, and it was hard to wrap his mind around that.

He already had so much more than he'd expected. He'd never let himself hope when he'd been alone in the forest. He'd always known Kari would eventually spread his wings and find his own life, and he'd been ready to be left behind. He should have known better. That wasn't like Kari.

"Forty-two isn't old," Kaspar pointed out.

"Maybe not, but I'm much older than most of the carriers here." He was older than *all* of them. Julian was the only one who was heading toward middle age, and he didn't mind it.

He'd lived his life. It might not have been a life most people would want, but it had been *his*, and in some ways, he'd been happy. He'd been able to raise his baby on his own and watch Kari become an adult. And now he could watch Kari fall in love and have his own baby.

That was what he'd wanted in life. He wanted his son to be happy and for himself to have a decent life. He did, now. He always would, or at least, he hoped so. He wasn't alone anymore. And he knew Kaspar was interested in him. He'd realized that, even though he'd never been in this situation, and he wasn't quite sure what to do about it. Kaspar might not think that forty-two was old, but compared to his twenty-five, it was. The years of difference meant that Kaspar could be Julian's son. Kaspar was the same age as Kari.

Julian liked Kaspar, even though he was trying his best to keep away from him. He couldn't risk it. Kaspar deserved so much more. Besides, they were both carriers. Carriers might be free now, but people would still raise some eyebrows if two carriers were together. Everyone was so used to carriers being sold and married to alphas that it would take some time for them to accept that they were more than just baby-makers. Julian already knew that, but that didn't mean he wanted to fight that fight. He'd already fought so much in his life. He wanted to rest now. He didn't want to be the poster boy for carrier freedom.

But that didn't have anything to do with Kaspar, did it? No, the only reason Julian was pushing him away was because of their age difference, and because once everything was over, Kaspar would go home, and Julian would stay here. He wasn't going anywhere, not with Kari and his baby living with the cete. Kaspar was a bear shifter, and unlike Julian, he had a home to go back to.

"Julian?" Kaspar asked.

Julian smiled at him, even though he didn't feel much like smiling. "Yes?"

Kaspar looked down at his sandwich, then back at Julian. "Forty-two years old isn't old."

"It's certainly older than you."

"What if I don't care? I mean, yes, you're older, but it doesn't mean you already have one foot in the grave. You're not old, Julian. You deserve your own life, just as much as Chris and Jacob do. We all do. You deserve to be happy."

"But I am. Don't you see? I never expected or hoped for everything I have now. I have a home and a family. I'm going to be a grandfather." He snorted. "If that's not what being old is about, then I don't know what is. And it's okay. I've lived my life, and I'm fine with that."

Kaspar shook his head. "Your life isn't over."

"You're right. I guess in some ways, it's only getting started." And no matter how old he was, Julian couldn't wait to see what the future held for him.

CHAPTER TWO

Kari was whining. It made Julian smile. He was used to it, but it was still a surprise. Kari had always prided himself on being strong and on not needing anyone. Yet now that he had a partner, a home, and a future, he finally allowed himself to relax — and to whine where other people might hear him.

Julian loved it.

He'd always wanted this for his son. Their life had been hard, and even though Julian hadn't been able to do anything about it, he'd prayed. He'd prayed that Kari would find a home, and he had. He'd prayed that Kari would find someone he could be himself with, and he'd met Calder.

"He hogs the blankets, Dad," Kari said.

Julian had to force himself not to smile. "And you're cold?"

Kari nodded. He was pouting, too, which was even more unusual than the whining. "I'm always cold these nights. Then during the day, I'm always too hot and sweaty."

"Why don't you put another blanket on the bed? Maybe keep it on your side, and if Calder steals all of the blankets, you can use that one. Wrap yourself into it like a burrito, and he won't be able to take it away from you."

Kari scowled. "But then I won't be able to unwrap myself every time I have to go to the bathroom."

"That's right. I forgot what it was like to be pregnant." It had been such a long time ago.

Julian had loved every second of it, even though Kari hadn't been put in his body willingly. He hated the memories of the rape, of course, but he loved his son, and he knew he'd made the right decision by running away and having him on his own. Still, he was grateful that Kari had more people in his life now. Julian's pregnancy and Kari's birth had been hell on Julian's body, and he'd been entirely alone for both. It was good that Kari had a healer he saw regularly and a partner.

Some days Julian wished he had someone who stole his blankets. Instead, he had his own bed, which he didn't have to share with anyone. No one stole his blankets. No one smiled at him sleepily in the morning. No one rubbed his shoulders when he was tired and they ached.

"What's going on?" Kari asked.

Julian blinked. "I don't know. You were saying that you had to get up often during the night to go to the bathroom."

Kari waved Julian's words away. "Not about that. I already know that's happening. I think I've gone to the bathroom already twenty times today. This baby is tip-tapping on my bladder, and I hate him."

Julian chuckled and patted his son's hand. "You don't hate him."

"I do." Kari sighed and rubbed his stomach. "You're right. I *don't* hate him. I just wish we could skip ahead to the birth and having a baby instead of looking like I swallowed a watermelon."

"You don't look like you swallowed a watermelon. Hell, you're barely showing as it is."

Kari scowled again. "I'm fat, Dad."

"You're not fat. You're carrying a baby. Calder's baby. Wait until you're eight months along. *Then*, you'll look like you swallowed a watermelon."

That made Kari smile for all of a second before he turned his attention back to Julian. "What were you thinking about just now? Before the watermelon thing."

Julian didn't want to talk about it. Kari was his son, and he'd always done his best to shield him from his feelings. Kari didn't deserve to have all of that dumped onto his shoulders. Julian was the father, and he was the one who needed to keep Kari happy, not the other way around. "I'm fine."

"You're not. Come on. I know we're not as close as we used to be now that I don't live with you anymore, but it doesn't mean you can't talk to me. I *want* you to talk to me. I'm an adult. I can take anything you want to tell me."

Julian shook his head and took one of the cookies from the plate he'd put together when Kari had arrived. He nibbled a corner, contemplating what to do. He *could* talk to Kari about this. As Kari had pointed out, he was an adult now, and he understood much more than he had when he was a teenager. "I'm happy for you," Julian started, unsure how to explain. "Even though Calder steals the blankets and does a lot of things that make you angry, you still have him. You love him, and he loves you, and you're building a family together. You've always been alone. You only had me. That's not the case anymore, and you should give yourself some time to get used to that"

Kari's eyes narrowed. "And?"

"And nothing. I'm happy for you, even though I still think I'm too young to be a grandfather. But I was listening to you talk about Calder, and I wished I had someone who stole my blankets, too. That's all." Julian looked away. He wasn't ashamed of feeling this way, but he and Kari didn't talk about these things, usually.

Kari's hand appeared in Julian's sight, and he squeezed one of Julian's hands. "You're lonely," Kari declared.

"Of course not. I share the house with more than a dozen people. I'm not lonely."

"But none of them wake up in your bed." Kari paused. "Or do they? What about Kaspar?"

Julian should have known the conversation would go that way. "What about him?"

Kari rolled his eyes. "Come on, Dad. I know you like him, and it's obvious he likes you, too. He could be the one who stole your blankets if you wanted."

Julian shook his head. "He might have a crush on me, but we both know it's not something we should indulge in. What's in it for him? I'm old and damaged. He's only twenty-five years old, and he could have anyone he wanted. Even if he decides he doesn't want to carry children, he can find someone to be with. Now that things are changing for carriers, people aren't going to see us as just baby-makers anymore." Although it would take time, and Julian was aware of that.

He was also aware of how his chest painfully squeezed when he thought of Kaspar being with anyone else.

"I don't think he wants anyone else. Every time you're in the room with him, he looks at you like you hung the moon. He likes you, and I think you should at least give him a chance." Kari paused. "And you are not damaged. Stop saying that. You're a good man, a man who hasn't had the easiest life, yet did his best so I could have a better life."

But Julian *was* damaged. It wasn't only his age, either. Carrying Kari and having him on his own had changed his body, and he would never get back what he'd had before. He would never get back the ability to have children—not that Kaspar needed him to. Kaspar was a carrier, too, and if he wanted children, he could carry them himself. But having lost that part of himself made Julian feel incomplete, and yes, damaged. He would never say that to Kari, though. It wasn't Kari's fault, and he didn't want his son to think it was.

He shook his head. "There are a lot of people better suited to Kaspar than I am. I accepted my fate a long time ago, Kari. You don't have to try so hard to make me happy. I already am, and I don't need Kaspar to be."

Kari threw his hands in the air. "I never said you needed

him to be happy, just that you would be happy with him. Come on, Dad. You like him, and he likes you. What are you waiting for?"

Julian shook his head again. "I can't do that to him. I told you. I'm old and damaged. I'm going to be a grandfather. I have everything I need and can handle."

Kari pushed away from the table and rose to his feet. He pointed a finger at Julian, who blinked at him. "I told you not to say those things about yourself. You are *not* damaged, Dad. You're just pigheaded. You don't want to see the truth. You might be my father, but it doesn't mean you're not a man, and you have eyes. Kaspar wants you, and if you don't let him in your life, someone else will notice him, and he'll get snagged from under your nose."

Kari stomped away and left the house, and Julian watched him go. He was more amused than anything at Kari's last words. Kari wasn't wrong, of course, but Julian wouldn't do anything about it.

He couldn't. Kaspar had all his life in front of him, while Julian's was already half gone. There was nothing he could offer Kaspar, and he wouldn't change his mind about that.

Kaspar straightened from his pose and tilted his face toward the sun. He smiled at how good it felt. God, he'd missed this. He'd never been forbidden to leave the Bishop House, but he and the other carriers had been careful. They hadn't wanted to risk it, which meant they had stayed inside as much as possible, just in case.

But now there were laws. Carriers were free to be out and about and to do what they wanted, just like everyone else in the forest. Kaspar had started doing his yoga in the morning outside only a few weeks ago, and it felt so good.

The front door slammed, making Kaspar jump. He looked

up, blinking at Kari, who was stomping his way down the porch steps. Kaspar expected him to make a beeline for his car parked in front of the house. No doubt he'd been here to meet with Julian, and from the looks of it, they'd fought.

Kaspar didn't think he'd ever spoken to Kari, not for long, anyway. They certainly weren't friends, which was why he was surprised when Kari turned toward him instead of going to the car. He never stopped stomping, and Kaspar wondered if he was about to get punched. He didn't think he'd done anything that would warrant that, but Kari was a little wild.

Kari stopped right in front of Kaspar and looked up at him. "You're an idiot," he spat out.

Kaspar blinked. "I'm sorry?"

"You're an idiot. What the fuck are you doing?"

Kaspar looked around. "I was doing yoga." He'd thought it was obvious. He was wearing yoga pants and a loose t-shirt, and he was standing on a yoga mat.

Kari's eyes narrowed. "That's not what I meant."

"I have no idea what you meant. If you want me to answer, you have to explain yourself." Kaspar didn't like to be yelled at, but especially not when he didn't understand why it was happening.

Kari rolled his eyes. "You need to make a move. I don't know, grab him and throw him on the bed, something like that. Have your wicked way with him. I don't like to think of him having sex, but I'm aware that's how I was born. Well, he was raped, so it's not the same thing, but he's a guy, and I'm a guy, and I know how it works. I might not want to imagine him in that kind of situation, and I'm trying hard not to, but I know it's going to happen eventually, and I think it would be good for both of you."

"I have no idea what you're talking about." Kaspar was almost afraid to tell Kari that. Kari looked convinced of whatever he was saying, and Kaspar was curious. He didn't want

Kari to get even angrier at him, though. He was known to kill people when he was angry.

Kari sighed, and his shoulders slumped. He cradled his small baby bump, and in just a second, he went from an angry, threatening guy to a sweet pregnant man. "My father. You're going to lose him if you don't take the first step."

That made more sense. Kaspar wasn't going to offend Kari by acting like he didn't know what he was talking about, not when he did. "I don't think he wants me that way."

Kari rolled his eyes. "Of course he does. It's obvious to everyone but you."

"He *told* me he doesn't want me."

Kari cocked his head. "So you talked to him about this?"

"No, but we talked about him having a second chance at life and about what he deserves after everything he's been through."

"Let me guess. He fed you some bullshit about him being too old and damaged."

Kaspar was amused rather than angry. No matter how Kari spoke, Kaspar knew he cared about his father. That was why he was talking to Kaspar in the first place. He might not be going at it the right way, but he *was* going at it, and he was trying to help. "He told me he was too old for me."

"I *knew* it. And the worst part is that he's convinced of that. You're what? Thirty?"

Kaspar rubbed the back of his neck, wondering if he should be offended. "Twenty-five."

Kari cringed. "Right. Sorry. I've never been great at guessing age. And okay, that's almost twenty years between the two of you, which is a lot. I don't think it matters, though, not when it's obvious the two of you are in love."

Kaspar's stomach felt like it dropped to the ground. "I never said anything about being in love."

"God, I'm rolling my eyes so much today between you and

my father that I expect them to just roll out of my skull and drop on the ground. You're right, you never said anything about being in love, but again, it's obvious to anyone who sees you. You look at him like he's the best thing next to chocolate, and let me tell you, there's nothing better than chocolate."

Kaspar wasn't sure what to make of that. He understood what Kari was saying, but Kari was scary. Kaspar could continue to deny everything, and he might have if he'd been facing anyone but Kari. He *was* facing Kari, though.

He shuffled his feet, hoping his next words wouldn't get him killed. "So what if I'm in love with him?"

Kari grinned. It was a bit feral, but it was a smile. "My father is a good man. He raised me on his own, and he made me the man I am today. He deserves the world. I know he's in love with you, and since he wants you, he deserves to have you. You have to do something about it."

"What do you want me to do? He was clear. He thinks he's too old and damaged for me."

"You don't, though. Right?" His expression made it clear that if Kaspar's answer was yes, he would end the day without his balls attached to his body. They would probably be hanging from Kari's neck.

Kaspar swallowed. "I don't care what happened to him. I don't care what happened to his body or why he thinks he's damaged. He's Julian. He's one of the sweetest and most gentle men I've ever known. And I am in love with him."

Kari gave Kaspar a triumphant smile. "I knew it. And since I was right, you know I'm right about this, too."

"Right about what?"

"That he's in love with you, too, and that you need to make a move. He's not going to make it. He'll never take the first step because just like you said, he thinks he's too old and damaged. You *have* to show him that neither of those things are true."

The thought was terrifying, though. Kaspar couldn't say he'd been rejected often, but that was because he'd been sheltered. He was a carrier, and Morris, his alpha, had always tried to keep him safe. And it had worked. Kaspar was here today only because Morris had made sure he could leave sleuth territory safely and spend as much time as he needed at the Bishop House. But that meant Kaspar didn't have a lot of experience with other men. He didn't have a lot of experience with pretty much anything, to be honest.

He wanted to get that experience, though, and he wanted to get it with Julian. Could he take that step? Could he ignore Julian's words and go full steam ahead?

Kari smiled, and he looked so much like Julian that he made Kaspar's heart beat faster. "I know that putting yourself out there is scary. I went through the same thing with Calder, and I might still be running if I hadn't gotten pregnant. But you have to trust people. You can't continue being alone in the world, and neither can my father. You both deserve so much more, and you can get it together. What would be better than that?"

"I know I'm not alone," Kaspar said.

"Maybe, but you can't deny that like almost everyone here, you've been keeping your distance. Yes, you talk with the other carriers and with the guards, you joke around and help them, but do you ever let any of them in? Or have you kept the walls up around your heart? I've been doing the same thing since I was old enough to understand that people could hurt me, and I still am. But I let Calder in, and you should do the same with my father. You won't find a man who will treat you better than him."

Kaspar suspected he was right, but he wasn't quite sure what to do with it. Could he really go to Julian and tell him he was in love with him?

He wasn't sure, but he supposed that he might be about to

find out.

"I just met Kari outside. Why did he storm out?" Kaspar asked as he walked into the living room, startling Julian.

Julian put down his book. He hadn't actually been reading, but rather, faking it. He'd been thinking about what Kari had told him instead, but he'd wanted people to leave him alone, and what better excuse than that he was reading? Of course, having a book in his hand didn't mean people wouldn't come talk to him. God knew some of the men he shared the house with didn't understand that one needed peace to read. He'd been interrupted more than once while he read, but by now, he'd told them off often enough that most of them had learned.

Kaspar hadn't, apparently.

Julian cleared his throat. "I'm not entirely sure." That was a lie, but Kaspar didn't have to know. "We were talking about how Calder hogs the blankets and how Kari always needs to pee."

Kaspar flopped onto the couch next to Julian and grimaced. "That's one thing I'm not looking forward to when I get pregnant. Is it true that you have to go to the bathroom every five minutes?"

Julian couldn't help but smile at the image of Kaspar pregnant. It would be a beautiful sight. "It depends. If the baby is leaning on your bladder, then it sure feels like it's every five minutes. It gets worse when the baby gets bigger, of course."

Kaspar grimaced and patted his flat stomach. "Well, I'm not planning on getting pregnant anytime soon, so I guess that's a good thing. Why did Kari leave, then?"

"I don't know. He's pretty touchy these days."

"I want to say it's the hormones, but I don't want to be rude."

Julian laughed. "More than the hormones, it's Kari. He's always been like this." Julian's smile faded. "I think it's because he grew up on his own. He had me, but it wasn't the same thing. He wasn't socialized as much as he should have been. I'm lucky he turned out the way he did." Some days, Julian wondered if there was more he could have done, or if he could have tried harder. He wanted to think the answer to that was *no*, but was that the truth?

"So he's okay?"

"I think he's overwhelmed. Everything is happening to him at the same time, and he has to wrap his mind around it. He's always been a solitary person, and now he has a new relationship, friends, a cete, and he's pregnant. It's a lot to take in in only a few months."

Kaspar slowly nodded. "I can see that." He looked like he wanted to say more, but to Julian's dismay, he didn't.

Julian wanted to know what was bothering Kaspar, but he didn't want to push. It wasn't his right. If Kaspar wanted him to know what was going on in his head, he would tell him. Otherwise, it wasn't Julian's business.

"What was it like?" Kaspar suddenly asked.

Julian frowned. "What was what like?"

"Being pregnant. Having a kid."

Kaspar wasn't the first carrier to ask Julian the question, but Julian was surprised. He hadn't expected it from Kaspar. "I'm not sure how it is for other people, but for me, it was hard."

"You didn't have the most normal experience, though."

"I didn't." And he didn't just think about the rape when he talked about that. "I was only a few weeks pregnant when I decided to run away. That means I spent the next nine months hidden in the forest. In the beginning, I roamed in my animal form to be sure that no one would find me. I moved a lot. Once I found a spot I thought would be safe, I decided to settle down. It took me several months to build my house and get things ready for Kari." Julian shuddered like he always did when he thought about Kari's birth.

He'd been lucky. He and Kari had both made it, and he hadn't needed a healer, or rather, even though he'd needed one, he'd managed to deal without. "Kari's birth was . . . hard. It's not something anyone should go through on their own, but I didn't have a choice." And it had left Julian scarred for the rest of his life.

But he could deal with that. He knew he could.

"Raising Kari on my own, especially in the middle of the forest, was as hard as his birth, albeit in a different way. Especially when Kari became a teenager and started leaving the house more often and for longer stretches of time. In the beginning, I was terrified. I had no idea what was going on in the rest of the forest, who was in power, or what happened to carriers. I didn't know how they were treated, and I knew there was a good chance that Kari would be one, too." Because being a carrier was genetic. If Kari's child was a boy, odds were that he'd be a carrier, too. The thought was as scary as it had been when Julian had been pregnant with Kari. Julian prayed that his son would never have to go through what he had gone through.

"But you let him go. You didn't tell him to stay home," Kaspar pointed out.

"I tried in the beginning, because he was only fourteen or fifteen. But he's an adult now. I wasn't going to lock him in the house. I never wanted that life for him. He doesn't deserve it. He deserves everything he found with Calder, and I'm glad he has it."

"You deserve all of that, too. You didn't deserve what was done to you or the way you had to live for so long."

"Maybe not, but I don't have to anymore, do I? I'm here, too, and even though it's not the same, I have you and the other carriers and a new family."

Kaspar looked thoughtful, and Julian waited. He knew Kaspar had questions. "Have you thought about having another baby?" Kaspar finally asked, shocking Julian.

Apart from Kari, no one had ever asked him that question. The healer had hinted at it, but it had been to tell him it wouldn't be a good idea.

"I can't have another child," Julian murmured.

"I know you're older than me, but not too old to have a child," Kaspar said.

Julian shook his head. "It's not because of that. It was Kari's birth. It was rough on my body, and the fact that I was alone made everything worse. I can't have other children because my body can't take it." Estelle, the healer, hadn't gone into details, and Julian hadn't asked. He hadn't wanted to know, and he still didn't. It wasn't like he was planning to have another child anyway. He was alone, whatever Kari thought about that.

"Shit. I'm sorry for asking. I shouldn't have," Kaspar said in a rush.

Julian shook his head and smiled. "Don't worry about it. I've managed to wrap my mind around it, and I'm okay." Truthfully, Julian had never thought about having a second child. He'd been too focused on surviving and on making sure his son did, too. Maybe he would have started to think about it now that he was free, but he couldn't, and that was okay.

"What happened to you wasn't fair," Kaspar said.

"It wasn't, but life rarely is, is it? Besides, it could have been so much worse. What happened to me wasn't fair, but in the end, it was worth going through all of it."

"Because you have Kari."

"Yes. I have my son, and I'm going to be a grandfather. Through Kari, I have Calder and the rest of the cete. It's a lot more than I ever expected to have, and I'm happy. I don't need another child."

But for the first time, the thought that he didn't *need* a child didn't settle right in Julian's mind. Having children wasn't about needing them, but wanting them, and Kaspar's question had made him realize that maybe, if he'd had the possibility, he would have wanted to give Kari a little brother or sister. But he'd missed his chance. That dream was out of his reach, and he had to settle for the ones he could get.

That was more than enough for now, and it would have to be enough for the rest of his life.

****

Kaspar hadn't expected this, and he couldn't help but feel sorry for Julian, even though Julian himself didn't seem to feel the same way.

Kaspar realized that Julian had had time to wrap his mind around things, but it couldn't be easy. Julian already had Kari, of course, but that didn't mean that he hadn't wanted other children, especially now that he was free and that he had access to a healer, that he had a home and a place where he belonged. He wanted to tell Julian how much he was hurting for him, but he knew that wasn't his place.

Julian sounded at peace, and it made Kaspar wonder if he should do this. Julian was convinced that he had everything he needed in the world—a home, a family, everything. Could Kaspar endanger his hard-earned peace only because he wanted to be with Julian?

He wanted to. There was no denying that. Was it the right thing to do, though? He wanted to say yes, but he knew that came from a place of selfishness. He was in love with Julian, and he wanted him.

A lot of people lived in the Bishop House, but it just wasn't the same. They were friends, and Kaspar would always cherish their presence in his life, but he found himself watching couples and feeling jealous lately, and he knew exactly why that was. He had feelings for Julian, but he hadn't acted on them, and he wasn't sure he ever would. He couldn't help but feel jealous that those couples could be together while he had to watch Julian from afar.

He rubbed his face. He had to say something, even though he didn't know what. "I'm sorry that happened to you," he eventually settled on.

Julian smiled at him. He was always smiling, and he was gorgeous. "Don't be. I was sorry for myself for a while, but I'm sure things are better this way. Besides, there's nothing I can do to change it, is there? I might as well focus on what I have."

Kaspar couldn't deny that was a good approach to life. "And you have a lot of things."

"I do. This might not be the life I dreamed of when I was a kid or the life I expected to have, but it's a good life, and I'm happy. You don't have to worry about me."

Kaspar knew that was impossible. He would always worry about Julian, even if nothing ever happened between them. He wanted to be with Julian, though. He wished he knew what Julian thought about that, but then, that was what Kari had been talking about. He'd told Kaspar to take the first step because Julian wouldn't. He'd told Kaspar that if Kaspar didn't at least try, he would never know what Julian felt for him, and he might lose him forever. What would be worse? Not knowing if there could be something between them, or giving it a try and being pushed away? It was scary, but next to what Julian had been through, it was nothing.

Kaspar wasn't sure he could say the words out loud, though. He wanted to, but when he opened his mouth, they got stuck in his throat.

Julian frowned and leaned closer. "Are you okay?" he

asked.

He was so gentle. He always worried about other people, including Kaspar. Kaspar had seen him do that every day since he'd arrived at the Bishop House, and everyone in the house loved him for it. Kaspar would never tell him that, because it would only reinforce his feeling that he was old, but a lot of the carriers, especially the younger ones who didn't have a father figure in life, saw him that way. Kaspar had heard a few of them talk, and he was glad they had him. He wasn't sure what Julian thought about it, but knowing him, he was happy.

That didn't solve Kaspar's problem right now, though. He licked his lips and looked at Julian, who looked even more worried. He cleared his throat and had to force the words out. "I'm fine."

"Are you sure? Because you don't look fine. Is there something wrong? Is it something I said?"

Kaspar shook his head and decided just to throw himself off the cliff. He leaned even closer and pressed his lips against Julian's, then jerked back as if they'd burned him. He knew his eyes were wide as he stared at Julian. Their expressions were probably similar, and Julian was shocked.

Julian touched his lips gently. "What did you do that for?" he asked.

Kaspar had wanted to avoid this conversation, but obviously, he wouldn't be able to. "Because I wanted to. Because I've been wanting to do it since you arrived here."

Julian frowned slightly. "You could have kissed anyone else. Why me?"

This was it. "Because I'm in love with you." Kaspar looked away. He didn't want to see the rejection if that was what would happen.

"You're in love with me?" There was something in Julian's voice, something vulnerable that felt like it might break if

Kaspar gave him the wrong answer. Kaspar hoped he wouldn't. He could only do what his heart wanted him to do and follow the path that was set for him.

"I am. I've been falling in love for a while. I've been watching you, and you're perfect."

Julian chuckled. "No one is perfect."

"Then you're perfect for me." It sounded corny, but it was true.

"We're both carriers."

Kaspar had known that would be a snag. "So? We're both human beings. We're both guys. What does it matter? We're free, remember? We can be with whoever we want, and no one can say anything about it. I love you, Julian. I've loved you for a while, and I'm sorry if I kissed you and you didn't want me to, but I love you and—"

Julian pushed into Kaspar's personal space, reaching for him. Their teeth bumped together, but Kaspar wouldn't have stopped for anything. Instead, he wrapped his arms around Julian and held him close as they kissed.

Julian had kissed him. Instead of stopping him or telling him that there never could be anything between them, he had kissed him, and he was still kissing him. Kaspar didn't know what it meant, if Julian shared his feelings or if he was feeling pity for him, but right now, he would take just about anything.

"We're crazy," Julian murmured.

"So?" Kaspar asked. He felt dizzy but in the best way. "We are *free*, remember? We can do this if we want." And Kaspar wanted to.

Julian wrapped his arms around Kaspar's neck. "I haven't felt this way in . . . ever, I think."

Kaspar wanted to protect Julian, even though Julian was older than him. But Kaspar's life had been easy, while Julian's hadn't. Kaspar would do everything he could to make Julian happy from now on, and he would make sure Julian knew that. If they felt the same way, they deserved to be together, whatever others said or thought. Kaspar didn't care, not as long as Julian wanted the same thing he did.

They kissed again, and Kaspar pushed all his thoughts away. Now wasn't the time to think. It was the time to feel, and it was the best feeling ever.

CHAPTER THREE

Things were fragile and delicate, but Kaspar was happy. He sighed and pressed himself closer to Julian, who chuckled and rolled to his back.

A few days had passed since their first kiss on the couch, and they'd moved their making-out sessions to Julian's bedroom. He had one of the few single rooms, because Kari had threatened to tear a few heads off if his father wasn't given a single. Kaspar hadn't understood why Julian should be privileged at the time, but now he was glad he was. Besides, he knew the other carriers in the house didn't mind. They looked up to Julian, and so did Kari. Kaspar was pretty sure that Kari still snuck in every so often at night to sleep with his father, and he thought it was sweet. Kari and Julian had only had each other for so long that he wasn't surprised they still needed each other that way.

But now Julian also had Kaspar, and Kaspar pushed closer to him again, wanting to kiss him some more. Julian laughed and shook his head. His cheeks were flushed and his hair was all over the place, and Kaspar felt smug that he'd been the one to do that. "Shouldn't we do something else?" Julian asked. "Something that isn't kissing?"

"Why? Kissing is good. I like kissing."

Truth to be told, Kaspar was terrified. They hadn't talked about this, but they'd been stealing moments since their first kiss. They had to talk. He knew that. They had to know what they wanted from each other and decide what the next step would be for them. It felt so good to be in the moment, though. Kaspar didn't have to think or worry. He could be with Julian and enjoy his presence.

"We should talk about what we want the others to know," Julian said. He didn't move away when Kaspar kissed him again, but Kaspar knew he was right, so he kept the kiss light.

"I don't want us to hide," he said. He didn't know a lot of things, but this, he was sure of. He had no idea what would happen between them, what their relationship would become, but he never wanted to hide Julian. After spending almost his entire life in hiding, Julian deserved to be shown off if that was what he wanted.

Julian's cheeks flushed harder. "Good, because I don't want to hide you, either. You're right. What we do isn't shameful, and we're free to do it. We shouldn't have to hide it."

"Then we won't." Kaspar grinned. "Will you be my boyfriend?"

Julian's smile could have lit up the sky. "I thought you'd never ask. Yes, I'll be your boyfriend."

Kaspar took one of Julian's hands and linked their fingers together. "It's official, then. You're my boyfriend."

Julian looked at their hands. His gaze had a touch of incredulity, as if he couldn't quite believe what he was seeing. "And you're mine," he said.

Kaspar's smile widened, and he leaned closer to kiss Julian again, but a knock on the door interrupted them.

Kaspar fought the instinct to jump away—even though Kari had told him to take the first step, there was no telling how he would react at finding Kaspar in his father's bed—but Julian kept him right where he was, not letting go of his hand. "Who is it?" he called out.

"There's a meeting downstairs," Burnell said.

Kaspar and Julian looked at each other. "What meeting?" Julian called out.

"No idea, but Thomas is there. So is Calder and your son. I'm gathering everyone. We'll be in the living room."

"Thank you."

They waited until they heard Burnell's footsteps fade away, then Kaspar asked, "What do you think this is about?"

"I don't know. It wasn't planned, that's for sure."

"Has something happened?"

"Maybe." They were isolated in the Bishop House, no matter how much the cete worked at making them comfortable. It didn't change the fact that they lived away from most of the cete and the other shifters in the forest, and that they were always the last ones to find out what was happening. It wasn't always a bad thing, but Kaspar didn't like feeling lost.

Julian sighed. "I suppose we should get up."

Kaspar kissed him one last time, then rolled off the bed. "We might as well go see what's happening."

He was curious. Meetings didn't often happen in the Bishop House, but especially not now that things were settling down in the forest. Maybe the alphas were here to retrieve their carriers. It was a possibility, and one Kaspar had expected to happen a while back. He'd thought that as soon as the council passed the new laws, alphas would start withdrawing the carriers from the house. Some had tried, but Kari had stepped in, and together, they'd all stood up so they would help the cete fight the coyotes.

But the danger had passed, and they'd settled back down into their lives. It was bound to change eventually, and sooner rather than later. That meant Kaspar would have to talk to Morris. He was Kaspar's alpha, but Kaspar wasn't worried, not the way Chris and a few others were.

Morris wouldn't care if Kaspar wanted to stay with the cete. It wasn't just because the sleuth and the cete had allied after the marriage between Levi and Demetri. Morris had always been a good alpha, and he would want Kaspar to choose his life. Still, the conversation wouldn't be an easy one for Kaspar. He'd always seen Morris as an authoritative figure, and that hadn't changed. The idea of talking to him made Kaspar slightly nervous.

"Ready to go?" Julian asked.

He was waiting at the door, and Kaspar moved toward him. He kissed him and opened the door, but to his surprise, Julian took one of his hands and twined their fingers together again as they stepped out in the hallway. Kaspar looked from their hands to Julian's face, then nodded.

They were doing this. They were officially together, and Kaspar couldn't have been happier.

They headed downstairs, and of course, everyone noticed their hands right away. They were teased a few times, but it wasn't mean. They were a family, and everyone was happy for them.

Well, everyone but Chris, who took one look at them and stomped his way to the other side of the room.

Kaspar didn't blame him. He might never have had his heart broken the way Chris had, but he could imagine how painful it was and that he didn't want to be anywhere close to the newest couple in the house.

Kaspar and Julian settled toward the back of the room. Someone had brought in several chairs so that everyone would have a place to sit. Of course, Kaspar and Julian sat next to each other.

Calder, Kari, Thomas, and his son Joel were at the head of the room, talking. Kaspar didn't miss the way Kari looked at him a few times, and he grinned when Kari winked at him. That was as much of a blessing as he would have.

Thomas cleared his throat as soon as everyone was in the room. "Thank you for coming," he started.

"It's not like we have anything better to do," Calum muttered.

Everyone was used to his bad moods, so they ignored him.

"I wanted to have a meeting because the council has decided something," Thomas said. "As you know, we now have the majority. We also have a few problems, though. The coyotes don't have an alpha anymore, and the human team is coming. I know it's a lot to digest, but it's nothing you have to worry about. The council has all of this in hand, and you can go back to your homes if you want to. The Bishop House will always be open for you, but I know that some of your alphas want to get you back to your own territory. Of course, feel free to stay if you don't want to go back."

"Will you stand up to our alphas if we decide to stay?" Chris asked.

There was a pause, and Kaspar held his breath. He didn't know how Thomas would answer, but it was important.

Thomas cleared his throat. "Obviously, I don't want to fight with any of the other alphas. With a human team coming, we need to be united now more than ever. But yes. You're an adult, as is everyone else here. If you want to stay and go against your alpha's wishes, I will support you."

The atmosphere in the room seemed to relax. Kaspar wasn't sure what this meant for Chris, but Thomas had given them the best answer he could have.

"There's something else," Thomas said. He looked around, and Kaspar held his breath. "The council decided during their last meeting that there needs to be a carrier member added."

Kaspar sat back. He hadn't expected that, and he wasn't sure what to make of it. "What do you think?" he asked Julian.

"That it's a good thing. It's about time carriers are represented. It's about time someone fought for them."

Calder stepped forward. "I know not every carrier lives here, but since the majority of you are in this room right now, we'd like to have a quick vote. You know each other better than anyone else. You know who you want to be on the council to represent you. So I'm asking for a name. We can vote and discuss this later if we need to, but this is where we start."

There was a moment of silence, then someone—Kaspar was pretty sure it was Chris—said, "Julian."

Julian had heard that wrong. He had to have, because he couldn't believe that someone wanted him to be a council member.

He looked around. Everyone was staring at him, which meant he probably *had* heard it right. He cleared his throat and opened his mouth to say something, but what? He had no idea what to say, what he was feeling, or even if he wanted the job.

Because that was what it was—a job, and an important one at that.

"Julian?" Kaspar asked softly.

Julian forced himself to look at him. "Yes?"

"What do you think of the idea? Chris thinks you would be the perfect council member to represent us in the council. Is it something you want to consider?"

"Why don't we take a vote?" Calder suggested.

Julian could have kissed him for taking the heat away from him for a few minutes. Instead, he stayed right where he was. He wasn't sure he could have moved even if he'd tried.

"Everyone here who wants Julian to represent them on the council, please raise your hand," Calder said.

Of course, everyone did. Julian looked at Kaspar again, and sure enough, his hand was up, too. Kaspar shrugged and gave Julian a little smile. "If you don't want the job, you can say no, but I do think you would be good at it," he explained.

Julian *wanted* to say no. He was pretty sure he wasn't the perfect person to take the job like everyone seemed to think.

He'd spent most of his life alone in the woods with only his son for company. Why did the carriers expect him to stand up for them in front of people who would no doubt hate him and would make it known what they thought about him being a carrier? They would see him as less than human, like someone who didn't belong, and they wouldn't be wrong about that last part. Julian didn't belong anywhere but with the other carriers.

"Julian?" Thomas asked. Julian blinked, surprised to see the alpha so close to him. Thomas crouched next to Julian's chair. He looked at Julian's hand, which was still linked with Kaspar's, but he didn't say anything about it. "You don't have to do this if you don't want to," he murmured. "I understand how big a responsibility it is. It was just a suggestion, and if you say no, we'll find someone else."

"Do you think I would be good at it?" Julian couldn't help but ask.

"Honestly? I think that once you get used to it and to the number of people you'll have to meet, you'll be *great* at it. You're a good man, and you know firsthand what happened to carriers in the past. But you're still standing, and you're strong. Besides, don't think I haven't noticed how you take care of the carriers in the house. You're behaving like an alpha, and that's why you *will* be a good council member. You want the best for them, and you'll work for that. You also won't be alone. Calder will be there, as well as other council members on our side. If you want, you can meet all of them before accepting. But the carriers seem to want you, and unless you're against this, I think it would be a good idea for you to accept the job. Also, the other carriers we know about are much younger than you."

Julian wasn't offended. He was the oldest in the house, and he didn't see it as a problem, even though sometimes, doubts poked at his mind. They were fairly easy to ignore most of the time, though. "But I'm old enough that the council members will respect me, at least for that. It will be one less strike against me." He already had a huge one since he was a carrier, and no matter how nice Thomas and the others were, not everyone would be.

Julian could imagine that some council members wouldn't be happy at having a carrier being their equal, not when they thought carriers were inferior—except when they bore children. They believed that was the only good thing a carrier could do, and it made Julian angry. He'd seen a lot of behavior like that when he'd lived with the weasel gang, and he knew it would never change until someone pushed.

He sighed. He wanted to say no, but he felt like he had to give back after everything Thomas and the cete had done for him and his son. Besides, he also wanted to protect the younger carriers. They were starting their lives, and they were starting it at a disadvantage because they could have children. Some of them had been horribly abused. Some already had children because they'd been raped. There wasn't much Julian could do for them, but *this*, he could.

He looked around. They were all looking at him, their faces so full of hope and trust. How was he supposed to say no? He'd thought he would spend the rest of his life here, taking care of Kari and his son or daughter, hopefully along with Kaspar, but it looked like fate had something different waiting for him.

"All right. I'll do it." The words spilled out, and he prayed he wouldn't regret them.

Thomas beamed and rose from his crouch. He offered Julian his hand, and Julian shook it with trembling fingers. "You won't regret it," he said. He paused and cocked his head. "Well, maybe you will. I know that some days I regret being the alpha, and I'm sure Calder feels the same way about being a council member. But whatever you need, we'll be here for you. Why don't you come with Calder and me to the office? We can have a private meeting about what the council will expect from you, what your duties will be, and about your bodyguard. You can bring Kaspar or Kari with you, of course."

Julian blinked. "Bodyguard?"

Thomas grimaced. "I think it's necessary. We all do. I'm not saying you're weak, but—"

"But I'm vulnerable. I don't know much about how things work out there. I've been alone most of my life, and I'm a carrier to boot, and people are bound to hold that against me. I understand." Julian wasn't sure what he would do with a bodyguard, but he wouldn't resist. He had no intention of putting his life in danger, not when he was finally living it.

He got up, and to his surprise, everyone in the room started to clap. His throat closed. He felt like he was about to cry. He didn't, though. Instead, he raised his chin high and ignored the prickling behind his eyelids.

"Thank you. I'll do everything I can to make you proud of me," he announced.

The clapping got even louder. Julian had to get out of there before he started sobbing like a baby in front of everyone. He was grateful when Kaspar squeezed his hand and pushed him toward Thomas. Julian wanted to ask him to come with him, but he didn't. It wasn't Kaspar's place. He wasn't a council member.

Julian was.

Dammit. It was going to take some time to get used to.

Julian followed Thomas and Calder out of the living room and into the office. It was small, which was why they hadn't held the meeting there. Julian flopped into one of the chairs as soon as the door was closed. His legs felt like rubber, and it was slightly hard to breathe.

Thomas chuckled and sat next to him while Calder leaned

against the desk.

"Do you have questions?" Thomas asked.

"Probably more than you can answer right now."

"That's understandable. We won't go into details right now because you probably need some time to get used to the idea of your new role. Why don't you take a few days to wrap your mind around everything and come up with a list of questions? Calder will give you his phone number so you can call him if you need anything. He's the best person to answer your questions."

Julian couldn't do anything but nod. "You said something about a bodyguard?" That felt like something he had to know right now. If he was going to put his life in his bodyguard's hands, he wanted to get to know them.

Thomas nodded. "Yes. Calder and I talked to the guards. As you know, we're going to start phasing them out since the carriers aren't in as much danger as before. I thought that having one of them with you would make you feel more comfortable since you already know them."

"Who?" Julian liked all of them. They'd been nothing but nice to him and the other carriers.

"Jacob volunteered."

That wasn't good, not for Chris anyway. The way he'd looked at Julian earlier made sense now. He was angry because Jacob was putting Julian before him, or at least, that was what it had to feel like to him. "He really wants to do this?" Julian wasn't surprised. It looked like Jacob was trying to put more distance between him and Chris, probably because Chris would leave soon, and Jacob wasn't planning on going with him.

"He does. Unless you have something against it, I think he's a good choice. He's trained, and he's serious about his job."

Julian nodded. "That's fine with me. I trust him."

Everything was moving too fast, though. Julian needed time to wrap his mind around everything before he got too overwhelmed.

"Talk to him," Thomas said. "I'm sure he can answer any questions you have about his job. And if you'd rather have someone else, that's fine, too. I'm sure he'll understand."

"Honestly, I don't know what I want right now."

Thomas laughed. "That's normal. Take a few days. We'll talk again soon."

Julian wasn't sure a few days would be enough, but it didn't look like he would have a choice.

Kaspar was so freaking proud of Julian, but he wasn't sure it was his place, so he kept his mouth shut about it. He doubted Julian wanted to hear any more about him being a council member anyway.

He'd been in shock since he'd been voted in, and even more so after the private meeting he'd had with Thomas and Calder. He'd come out of the office looking dazed, and Kaspar had taken his hand and dragged him to his bedroom. They were both in bed right now, with Kaspar playing big spoon, Julian wrapped in his arms. He hadn't said anything yet, and Kaspar hadn't asked. If Julian wanted to talk, he just had to open his mouth and let the words out.

The silence was a bit heavy, though. Kaspar didn't mind it, but he wished he could ask the questions that pressed on his mind.

"Will you stop wiggling?" Julian suddenly asked.

Kaspar froze. He hadn't even noticed he was moving. "Sorry."

Julian chuckled.

Kaspar couldn't see his face, but he knew he was smiling, and he felt better.

"Don't be sorry. It's okay. It's just a bit unnerving." Julian unhooked Kaspar's arms from around him and turned around until he faced Kaspar.

Kaspar hugged him again as soon as he was settled. Julian would have to ask him to stop holding him if that was what he wanted.

"What's going on?" Julian asked.

Kaspar bit his lower lip. "I don't expect anything from you."

Julian arched a brow. "I'm sorry?"

Kaspar huffed. "I'm not the greatest when it comes to talking to people. I haven't spent most of my life in the woods like you did, but even when I was with the sleuth, Morris kept me isolated for my own good. I had friends and even a few boyfriends, but I'm awkward on the best of days, and you know it."

Julian's teasing expression softened. "I'm sorry. I didn't mean to hurt you."

"You didn't hurt me. It's just frustrating sometimes when I can't say what I mean to say without making a mess."

Julian cupped one of Kaspar's cheeks. "You don't have to worry about that when you're with me. I understand better than most people. Just take a deep breath, think about it, and I'll still be here waiting for you when you're ready to say whatever is on your mind."

Kaspar sucked in a breath and did what Julian had ordered. "I just wanted to know how you were feeling, but I didn't want you to think that you *had* to give me an answer."

"You want to know about the meeting."

"I do. I'm not surprised the carriers chose you, but I know this can't be easy for you. I'm surprised you accepted so readily, to be honest."

Julian relaxed against the pillow. "Honestly, I'm not sure what happened. I don't know what I'm doing. I can barely speak to people. I lived on my own for years, and I am the least sociable person you will ever meet. I have no idea where to start being a council member."

"Yet you said *yes.*"

Julian smiled. "I did. I know I could have said no, and I considered it. But then I looked around, and I saw you and everyone else. You were counting on me. For whatever reason, you have faith in me, and I need to honor that. Besides, I want the forest to be a better place for my grandson or granddaughter. I want them to be able to grow up to be whatever they want, and the best way to make that happen is to be right there on the council. I'm doing this for my family, but also all the other carriers in the forest. Kari had to hide, but I want to make sure he'll be the last one who has to do that."

"He still hasn't told you if it's a boy or girl?" Kaspar teased. He was mildly surprised. Julian and Kari were close, much closer than Kaspar had ever been to his parents.

Julian rolled his eyes. "I don't think he knows himself. Or rather, he's convinced it's a boy, but of course, he can't be sure yet."

"How much longer before he can?"

"Well, it depends on the position the baby is in. If he's lucky, he'll be able to find out in a few weeks. But if he's not, he could have to wait until the birth, although I think that's rare. I don't really have experience with that, though."

Right. Because Julian's pregnancy hadn't been monitored by a healer. He hadn't seen Kari when he was still inside him. He hadn't known that Kari was a boy until he'd given birth.

Kaspar was grateful Julian didn't get angry when he mentioned his past, because otherwise they probably would have already broken up at least a few times. Kaspar was curious about how Julian had survived in the forest, but even though he was trying his best not to be an asshole and not to ask too many questions about that, sometimes, he said things he shouldn't.

He rubbed a hand down Julian's back. "I'm not surprised you were the one who was chosen."

"No?"

"Well, I was a bit in the beginning. But it makes sense."

"It does?"

Kaspar laughed. "Are you fishing for compliments?"

"Not really. I'm trying to understand. I told you. I'm completely lost, and I don't know where to start. I don't know why people have this much faith in me."

"It's because *you* have faith in *them*. It's because they know you. It would have been so easy for you to isolate yourself when you arrived here. No one would have blamed you if you'd pushed everyone away. But instead, you act a bit like a father figure. Most of us are much younger than you, and even though Chris is angry with you, he knows that you're a good man. He was the one who nominated you, after all. He's nineteen, and while he does have a father, don't think I don't know how the two of you talked about Jacob."

Julian grimaced. "Way to make me feel old."

"You're not old. Older, sure. But not old." Kaspar kissed Julian's forehead. "And Chris will forgive you eventually. It's not like you did anything. He didn't force Jacob to become your bodyguard, or to not move with him to bobcat territory."

"I know. But I don't like for anyone to be angry with me."

"It will pass. Things are hard for him right now, and they will continue to be hard for a while, but it'll be over eventually, and Chris will make his peace with the situation." He'd have to, unless he wanted to leave the Bishop House angry with Julian, and Kaspar didn't think that was the case.

"What about you?" Julian asked.

"What about me?"

"We're talking about Chris leaving, and it made me realize that the same goes for you. Are you getting ready to go home?"

Kaspar shook his head. "I'm already home."

"You're a bear shifter. You're not home. The sleuth is your home."

"And it's now allied with the cete. I know Morris won't protest when I tell him I want to stay here."

"And that's what you want to do? Stay here?"

"Of course. I want to see where things can go between us. I'm not leaving you, Julian, especially not now that you need me the most. I'm staying at the Bishop House with you and the other carriers. It's not even because of you, but rather because it feels safer and like the other carriers might need me." It was probably wishful thinking, but the carriers had become Kaspar's family since he'd arrived here, much more than the sleuth and his own family. They gave him a sense of belonging he hadn't had with family. Kaspar's family loved him, and they always would, but they'd always kept him separated. He was a carrier, and he wasn't like them.

But he was like Julian and the other carriers.

Kaspar kissed the tip of Julian's nose, smiling when he wrinkled it. "I'm not going anywhere," he promised. "I hope you weren't planning to get rid of me anytime soon, because that won't happen." If Kaspar had anything to say about it, Julian would *never* get rid of him.

CHAPTER FOUR

This was it. It was Julian's first official meeting as a council member, and he couldn't stop bouncing his knee. He was sitting between Calder and Abel, and he couldn't help but stare at the door. The human team was about to come in, and he had no idea what was going to happen.

He hadn't left badger territory since he'd arrived at the Bishop House. Hell, he hadn't left badger territory since he'd moved there when he was seventeen and pregnant. He'd taken a risk by moving away from weasel territory and entering the territory of the bears and the badgers. He'd lived on the edge of both territories for so long that he'd been stunned when he'd arrived in Northwood this morning.

Everything was so different from when he was seventeen.

There were so many buildings, so many people, and so many *cars*. He hadn't known where to look, and it had been overwhelming. It still was. Even the council building was full of people and noises, and it made Julian slightly dizzy.

"Are you okay?" Abel asked in a murmur.

Julian straightened his back. He didn't want to show any kind of weakness, especially with more than a few council members glaring daggers at him. He knew that with him on the council, the majority was even more pronounced. He was on the good side, and they weren't happy about it. They weren't happy about his presence there, period. They didn't want a carrier, someone they saw as little more than a baby maker, making decisions with them, sitting next to them, and having the same privileges they did. That shouldn't be the case, since women sat on the council, too, but carriers had always been treated differently. Even though having a baby with a carrier was seen as a good thing, the carriers themselves were considered even lower than women.

Julian raised his chin. Being a carrier didn't define him. First of all, he was a human being and a man. He was a shifter, just like everyone else in the room. He deserved to be there. He'd been voted in, something none of the other people around the table could say. They'd all been chosen by their alpha, and while in some cases it had been a good thing, because they were good people, in others, Julian could have done without meeting them. Living with the carriers meant he'd heard a lot of the abuse that had been done to them — both by their alphas and their council members — and he had to resist the urge to snap at them. Especially those who were looking down at him like he was something nasty on the bottom of their shoes.

A knock on the door made Julian jump. He swallowed, looking around to make sure no one had noticed. Of course, someone had, but it was only Abel, and he pressed a hand to Julian's arm, smiling at him.

Julian couldn't help but ask. "How do you do this?"

Abel shrugged. "It's not easy. I had to decide that I could ignore what most people think about me. I'm not a carrier, but I'm a deer shifter, and you know what most predator shifters think about us. In the beginning, a few of them looked at me like they wanted to eat me, and not in a good way. But I knew nothing would happen. They might try to corner you when you're alone, and they might insult you and think you don't belong here, but they're wrong. That's what you have to focus on. You're here to do good, and that's what you're going to do, because you're that kind of man."

Julian wished he had as much faith in himself as Abel did, but he nodded and turned his attention back to the door. A guard had entered and was talking with another council member, who nodded at him. The guard stepped back to the door and opened it wider, and a man came in.

Julian had never met a human being before, but they didn't seem to be any different from shifters. He didn't think there had been a human in the forest for several decades, and he leaned forward, staring at the small group of people who entered the room.

The leader—and he had to be the leader—was tall and broad-shouldered, with dark hair and dark eyes. He looked at each and every single council member waiting for him without showing fear or revulsion. Julian hadn't known what to expect. Shifters were stuck in the forest because that was where humans had put them. They could have killed them, but instead, they had made them prisoners. They might have an entire forest to run around in, but that didn't change the fact that they couldn't leave.

But it wasn't these humans' fault. They might not even have been alive when shifters had been locked in. Julian needed to remember that, and to remember that he couldn't hold the fact that they were humans against them, just like people shouldn't hold the fact that he was a carrier against him.

Marjory, the bear council member, rose from her chair. "Welcome," she said. "Please take a seat."

They obeyed silently. Julian could see that the humans were nervous now. Their gazes kept bouncing from one person to the other, then to the door and windows. He suspected they expected to be attacked, and they were right to be worried. They might be armed to the teeth, but they were still human, and there was little they could do against a bear shifter.

But Marjory wouldn't attack them. No one would. It wasn't just because they would be in trouble with the humans outside the forest, either. They'd been left alone until now, but that wouldn't continue if they attacked and killed an entire human team.

They needed to stay safe.

The leader settled into one of the chairs right across the table from Julian, and Julian stiffened.

"My name is Luther," the man said. His voice was deep and graveled.

"I'd give you the names of everyone in the room, but as you can see, they're written in front of them. We thought it would be easier for you than to have to remember everyone," Marjory said. "I'm Marjory, the bear shifter council member."

Luther nodded. "You know why we're here?"

"Not exactly. We were told that a human team was being sent, but we weren't given details."

"There was an explosion."

Julian briefly closed his eyes. He could too easily remember that moment. He hadn't been anywhere near Thomas's house when it had exploded, but Kari had been, and Julian had been terrified. Luckily, his son had come out of it alive and in one piece.

"We've had . . .some problems with a few shifter groups," Abel said. His voice was soft, but there was a hint of steel in it. "The coyotes attacked the badgers."

Luther looked at the cards in front of everyone. Julian's had his name and the word *carrier* because that was who he represented, and he noticed Luther's gaze stopping on it. Luther didn't ask what it meant, though, and Julian was relieved.

"Why did they attack?"

"That is *not* your business," Jacqueline snapped. She was the coyote council member. No one wanted her here, but until a new alpha replaced her, she wasn't going anywhere, and she was using her power. She would milk this situation for as long as she could.

Calder cleared his throat. "It was an internal struggle. They had problems with the badgers. I'm sure you can appreciate the fact that we don't want to go into too many details."

"The only reason you all live here is that we allow it," Luther pointed out.

"Of course. But you have shown no interest in us for several decades. I find it odd that you do now."

Luther leaned back in his chair. "Are you implying something?"

"I'm not implying anything. I'm just saying that while the coyote and the badgers have fought, it's over now. The explosion was an accident. The house is already being rebuilt, and the coyote alpha has been dealt with. You have nothing to worry about. Even though you might not believe it because we're *animals*, we have things in hand. The forest is our home, and we don't allow people to disrupt our peace."

Julian held his breath. He expected Luther to snap and get angry, but instead, he slowly nodded. "I see. I still want more details, please."

He waited, and Julian could tell they were in for a very long meeting.

Kaspar was nervous when Julian came home, but he shouldn't have been. Julian trudged in, followed by Jacob. They both looked tired, but Julian especially so.

Kaspar rushed out of the living room. "Why don't you come sit down?" he told Julian. After Julian had taken his shoes off and left them at the bottom of the stairs, Kaspar gently steered him toward the living room.

He glared at everyone when he and Julian entered.

Hector jumped up from his spot on the couch so Julian could sit, then headed to the kitchen, saying, "I'm going to put together a tray for him."

Kaspar's heart swelled with love. These men might not be

his blood family, and they might not be related, but they were family. Nothing would ever change that. They took care of each other, and that was all that mattered. They were a better pack than most of the groups the carriers had been born into.

Julian settled on the couch. Kaspar sat next to him, and even though he wasn't sure what Julian thought of PDA, he wrapped an arm around his shoulders and pulled him close, kissing his temple.

"What happened?" Chris asked. He was staring at Julian, and definitely *not* looking at Jacob, who was hovering at the entrance of the living room.

Those two still hadn't made peace, and Kaspar wasn't sure they would at this point. Jacob had taken a job that meant he wouldn't go with Chris when Chris left, and Chris hadn't taken it well.

"Everything is fine," Julian said. He sucked in a breath and straightened, giving Kaspar a grateful smile and taking one of his hands to twine their fingers together. "We met with the human team."

"What do they look like?" Nico asked.

Julian smiled. "Like us. They're no different from us except for the fact that they can't shift into an animal. But when you meet them, they're just like us. And I think we got lucky. Even though the leader especially looked uncompromising, I think he's a good man. He asked questions, and he listened to what we had to say about what happened. He didn't make any rash decisions."

Chris snorted. "That you know of. But he could be telling his bosses that we deserve to die."

Julian gave him an indulgent smile. "He could, but I don't think he will. I'm not sure what's happening outside of the forest, but I doubt most human beings would want us to die. We might be different, and we might be their prisoners, but all of this happened decades ago."

Kaspar wasn't sure how much faith he had in human beings, but he supposed Julian knew the situation better than he did.

"Did you talk to the council about us?" Burnell asked. He was curled into an armchair, his arms around his legs.

"A little. But our situation has nothing to do with the council, not anymore. Thomas told me again as we came back that we are all free to stay if we want to."

There was a moment in which everyone seemed to look at everyone. Chris huffed. "Well, we know that Nico and I aren't staying, no matter how much we might want to."

"*I'd* like to stay, though," Burnell said. "I don't have a place to go to."

Some of the carriers in the room were here because their alphas had been abusing them, so Kaspar understood. He was one of the lucky ones. Morris had never raised a finger against him, and he'd made sure no one else did. Kaspar had never been attacked or abused, and the only reason he was in the Bishop House was that it had been too dangerous for him to stay with the sleuth when the council was hunting carriers. If he wanted, he could go home.

But he didn't want to.

He knew most of the people around him felt the same way. Even though they'd come here because they were in danger, this had become their home, and the other carriers had become their family. Some of them would have to leave because their alphas wouldn't want them to stay, but Kaspar suspected that most of them would stick around.

He was grateful. He wasn't sure how things would work now that they could leave the Bishop House and live their lives, but he understood that staying was familiar. It was safe. It was a home they could always come back to. It was better than throwing themselves out there not knowing what would happen, especially with some of the experiences they'd had.

"Can we really stay?" Josiah asked.

"You know you can. Has Thomas ever lied to you?" Kaspar asked. "Because he's never lied to me. I know I'm one of the lucky ones here, but I'm not going anywhere, either. This place has become my home, and I think the same goes for most of you."

"I could do without Redley leaving his socks all over the place, though," Lennox said.

Everyone laughed, and the tension was gone.

"Socks notwithstanding, we're all free to go or stay if we want," Julian repeated.

He got to his feet and stretched. He looked tired, and Kaspar wasn't surprised. He hadn't left the territory for more than twenty years. He hadn't met that many people for just as long, and he'd never had this kind of responsibility weighing on his shoulders. Today had to have been exhausting for him.

Kaspar got to his feet, too. Hector came into the room with the tray just then, and Kaspar took it from him, smiling gratefully. "Thank you. I think Julian wants to eat in his bedroom. He's tired."

There were murmurs of assent, and Kaspar gently knocked his shoulder against Julian's, then tilted his chin toward the entrance in what he hoped was an obvious gesture of *let's go*.

Julian looked around, hesitating. "If you need anything, feel free to come to me," he said.

"Go get some rest," Nico said. "We'll be here when you wake up. You deserve some sleep."

"And some loving from Kaspar," Chris added.

Once again, people laughed, and Kaspar smiled at Chris, who, surprisingly, smiled back. Chris was angry and bitter, but he was mature enough to understand that what was happening was no one's fault. He might snap and glare, but in the end, he would do what was right. He really was the best person to eventually replace his father at the head of the bobcat pride, no matter how much he resented that decision.

Kaspar and Julian headed upstairs, and they went straight to Julian's bedroom, just like they always did. Kaspar shared his room, and he was sure his roommates were grateful not to have him around as much as before. They might all want to stay here, but it didn't mean the Bishop House couldn't sometimes feel small with so many people living here.

"Everything really went well?" Kaspar asked as he put the tray down onto the small desk in the corner.

Julian closed the door and rubbed his face. "It did. I think I'm tired because it was so overwhelming more than anything, because I didn't really do anything. I was sitting most of the day, after all."

Kaspar went to him and gathered him into his arms, kissing the top of his head. "You're not used to this."

Julian chuckled. "And I'm old."

"You're not old. I'm going to have to fine you every time you say that if you continue."

Julian chuckled and looked up at him. "Fine me? And what does the fine consist of?"

"I don't know. Maybe a kiss? I wouldn't mind being kissed every time you say you're old." Or any time, period. Kaspar loved kissing Julian. He would be happy even if that was the only thing they did for the rest of their lives.

Julian shook his head. He was still smiling, and it was soft and gentle. "You don't have to fine me to get kissed. I *want* to kiss you."

"You never have to ask. Kiss me as many times and for as long as you want. I'll always be up for that." And for so many other things, but now wasn't the time to talk about them. Now was the time to take care of Julian and make sure he ate and got rest, and that was exactly what Kaspar did.

Chapter Five

This was the most complicated thing Julian had ever done, and he'd had a baby on his own.

He scratched the back of his neck and forced himself to listen to Calder, who was explaining how Julian was supposed to file paperwork. Julian had gotten lost when he'd started explaining *what* he was filing, and he wasn't about to ask.

He should know better. He was older than Calder, and he felt a bit ashamed that he couldn't follow his explanation, even though he knew it wasn't entirely his fault. He wasn't used to this kind of work, and no matter how hard he focused, he kept missing things that would probably be obvious for anyone else.

"—and again, if you need any help, feel free to ask me or anyone on our side of the council," Calder said.

Julian realized he was done explaining whatever he'd been explaining. "I'm really sorry, but I don't think I remember even fifty percent of what you just said," Julian confessed.

To his surprise, Calder laughed. "No worries. It's complicated. It was for me, too, and I didn't have the same experiences you had. We didn't ask you to become a council member so you could file paperwork. We want you in on the council meetings, mostly. We want you to be a voice for the carriers."

Sometimes Julian still felt a bit awkward with Calder. He was his son-in-law and a fellow council member. Although, being honest with himself, Julian felt awkward with a lot of people. He just wasn't used to being around other human beings.

"I feel like an idiot," he said.

"You're not. You're a very strong and intelligent man. You and Kari wouldn't have survived otherwise. And like I said, this is pretty complicated even for people who lived with the cete or any other shifter group for their entire life. Don't worry too much about it. If you need anything, just ask me. As long as you're here for the meetings to stand up for the carriers, everything will be all right."

He might be right, but Julian *wanted* to learn. If this was going to be his job, he needed to know what he was doing. He couldn't rely on Calder or anyone else for much longer. He'd never relied on anyone, and he wasn't going to start now.

The door of the meeting room opened, and Luther, the human leader, stepped in. He looked around the room, and his gaze stopped on Calder and Julian.

Julian resisted the urge to shift and hide under the table. Luther was an intimidating man, even though Julian was pretty sure he was a good person. He'd acted like one, anyway. Of course, Julian wasn't the best at evaluating people and guessing whether they were good or bad, but he trusted his instincts. They'd kept him alive since he was seventeen, and they would continue to.

"Can we help you?" Calder asked.

"Actually, yes. Can I talk to you?"

Julian's eyebrows rose high on his forehead, and he looked at Calder. He was surprised how polite Luther was. A few of his team members definitely weren't, and Julian suspected they saw shifters as little more than animals. Luther didn't seem to feel the same, and that was a relief.

Calder gestured at one of the chairs on the side of the table at which they were sitting. "Feel free."

Luther sat in one of the chairs. "I'd like more information about the coyotes."

Julian leaned back in his chair. He knew what had happened because he'd been told, but Calder had been right there. He would be better at answering Luther's questions than Julian would be.

"Let's hear it," Calder said.

Luther nodded and took out a small notebook from his pocket. He flipped a few pages, then asked, "I went over the reports of what happened in badger territory. I know you're already rebuilding."

"We are."

"And that's good. I was just wondering what the council will do about the coyotes."

Julian looked at Calder. He was curious about that, too. He had a few ideas, but he didn't think they mattered.

"There's not a lot we can do," Calder said cautiously. "The council doesn't have a say in who the next alpha will be. The various shifter groups are led autonomously."

"So you're going to leave the coyotes without an alpha? Will you hope that the next alpha won't try to blow you up?"

Calder bristled, and Julian could tell this wasn't going to end well if he didn't intervene.

It was terrifying, but he had to do it. "Usually, the next alpha is the heir," he explained.

"So did this alpha have children?" Luther asked.

Julian shook his head. "He was himself the son of the older alpha who died recently."

"Who's next, then? Does he have any brothers or sisters?"

Julian liked that Luther had assumed a woman could become alpha. He hoped that eventually that would become a reality, but he knew it was a battle they would need to fight later.

He looked at Calder again. "There's Josiah," he said.

"Who's that? A brother?"

"Yes. I'm pretty sure he won't want to be the alpha, though.

He was severely abused by his father and his older brother. In theory, he should be next, but he will probably decline." And that was apart from the fact that the coyotes might not want him as their alpha, since he was a carrier.

Julian didn't say the last bit out loud, though. Josiah wasn't here, and Julian didn't want to give away his secrets. Carriers might be free in the forest now, but that didn't mean they weren't still in danger, and there was no way to know what the humans would think about men being pregnant. It was fairly normal for shifters, but Julian could remember from what he'd learned when he was a kid that it wasn't for humans.

Luther put down his notebook. "Well, you're going to have to find a solution. I know it's none of my business, but I was sent here to keep an eye on the shifters and to make sure everything runs smoothly."

"You were sent to make sure we don't leave the forest," Calder snapped. He swallowed. "I apologize for my tone."

The corner of Luther's lips curled in a half-smile. "It's not a problem. And you're right. My bosses thought that you guys might be starting up a revolution or something like that. They were relieved to find out it was just a war between two shifter groups, but they were clear. They want the forest to be at peace, or they will intervene with force. You don't want that, and I don't, either. So whoever this next alpha will be, it has to be someone who won't start a war. It has to be someone that can work with the council and the other shifter groups. This is none of my business, but it's my advice."

He wasn't wrong. The coyotes and some of the other shifter groups were on the wrong side of all of this. They wanted things to stay the way they had for the past few decades, but that couldn't work. The shifters in the forest might be isolated from the rest of the world, but they needed to evolve, and that wouldn't happen if they stuck with old traditions, like the one of marrying carriers off to the best offer.

That was out of Julian's job description, though. He might be a council member now, but he couldn't select an alpha, and neither could the rest of the council. They couldn't make any promises to Luther, but when Julian looked at Calder, he knew they would try to talk to Josiah anyway.

Julian wasn't looking forward to it. He thought Josiah deserved to live the rest of his life the way he wanted after everything he'd gone through at the hands of the people who should have loved him. He hated the gang. His father and his brother were dead, but other people, people who had watched from afar and hadn't raised a finger when he was abused, were still there.

This could either go well or go terribly wrong. If Josiah declined to take the role of the alpha, they might be able to find a solution. If he agreed, though, they would need to keep an eye on him. He was a good man. Julian knew him well enough to be sure of that. That didn't mean that if he was in a position of power over the people who had hurt him, he wouldn't use it to hurt them back.

Julian had no way to know what would happen, but they needed to find a solution. Otherwise, the humans would step in, and *that* would definitely go wrong.

Kaspar smiled when he saw he'd gotten a text from Julian. It was weird to be in the house without him around. Julian hadn't been with them for long, but Kaspar had already gotten used to his presence, and since they'd started dating, he wanted to spend as much time as possible with him.

But Julian had a job now. He represented the carriers on the council, and it took a lot of time and energy from him. Kaspar was slightly dismayed, but he was also proud, and he would never say anything against the job. He knew Julian hadn't been excited at the thought of being a council member, but he had said yes, and he was working his ass off to make sure he succeeded.

Kaspar blinked when he read the text. He'd thought Julian was just checking in, but instead, he was telling him that he, Calder, and probably Thomas, were headed to the Bishop House to talk to Josiah. Kaspar wasn't sure what they wanted from him, but he could imagine.

Josiah was a coyote shifter, and the coyote band was without an alpha. It wasn't merely that, of course. Josiah's father and his brother had both been alphas. They'd been horrible, but that didn't change the fact that they'd been in charge and that usually, the next in line for the position was the other son.

Kaspar didn't know a lot about Josiah's life with his family. He did know that now that his father and brother were dead, he was alone in the world, at least when it came to blood-related people. He had a family with the other carriers, of course, but it wasn't the same thing. It was *better*, considering how abusive Josiah's blood family had been.

But being the alpha's son and brother meant that technically, Josiah was the next in line. There had never been an alpha carrier in the forest until now, and Kaspar wasn't sure people were ready for it. It would be a great thing, but between how bigoted some people were and what Josiah had gone through, Kaspar wasn't sure it would be a good idea.

But it wasn't his business. He wasn't a council member, and his opinion didn't count. He'd only been asked to find Josiah and bring him to the office if possible, so that was what he would do.

He headed to the kitchen. Josiah spent a lot of time there cooking. He had discovered a love for food when he'd arrived at the Bishop House, and no one had protested. Not only was he a good cook, but it also gave him peace. Kaspar didn't understand why, although it was probably because he himself hated cooking. But whatever worked for Josiah, it was good, especially if it meant the rest of them didn't have to take turns cooking anymore.

But the kitchen was empty, at least of Josiah. Redley and Hector were at the counter, though, their heads close as they talked quietly.

Kaspar cleared his throat. "Have you seen Josiah?" he asked.

Redley gestured at the door. "I saw him leave through the back door. He's probably still outside."

"Thanks." Kaspar headed to the door and slipped outside. He looked around, his eyebrows rising when he saw the bundle of clothes at the bottom of the porch steps.

He knew Josiah shifted. They all shifted, usually together, because it was fun. But Josiah always kept to himself, especially when he shifted. Kaspar didn't like it, but he hadn't pushed until now. He wasn't sure he should push at all.

He climbed down the porch steps and stood there, unsure what to do next. "Josiah?" he called out.

The bushes to his left rustled. A muzzle poked out of them, and Josiah appeared, looking terrified even in his coyote form. He lowered himself onto his stomach and dragged himself closer, and Kaspar took a step back, horrified. Was Josiah afraid of him? Or had something happened?

Josiah froze, and Kaspar realized that by taking that step back, he'd probably shown Josiah he was afraid of him. Nothing could be further from the truth, so he rushed toward Josiah's small coyote form, kneeling next to him. He reached for him to stroke his fur but stopped before he could touch Josiah.

"Can I touch you?" he asked. He didn't want to startle Josiah or to do something Josiah didn't want.

Josiah twisted his head to look at Kaspar, and Kaspar waited, his hand already raised. When Josiah finally nodded, Kaspar lowered his hand to the top of his head and rubbed. It took a few seconds for Josiah to relax, but when he did, he closed his eyes and seemed to enjoy the rubbing thoroughly.

Kaspar couldn't help but wonder how long it had been since someone had touched him, both in his human form and in his coyote form. He suspected that Estelle, the cete healer, was the last one who'd touched Josiah's human body, which wasn't great. And what about his coyote one? It had been a while since he'd last been with other coyotes, but even when he'd been with them, he'd been isolated and abused. He'd probably never been touched in a nice way when he was in this form, and Kaspar wished he could help with that. Maybe he was, but it didn't feel like enough.

"I have to talk to you," he said quietly.

Josiah's eyes flew open, and he looked at Kaspar.

Kaspar wasn't sure what to tell him, so he stuck with what he knew for sure. "I got a text from Julian. He's coming back, along with Calder. They want to talk to you. And no, I don't know about what. But they sent me to find you and bring you to the office if you're feeling up to it."

Josiah hesitated. Kaspar fully expected him to say no, or at least, to shake his head since he couldn't speak right now, but instead, he rose to his feet. Kaspar snatched his hand away, hoping he hadn't offended or scared Josiah. Josiah turned toward him, and Kaspar's eyes widened when he felt a wet and cold nose against his cheek. He wasn't sure what this was—a kiss, maybe—but he beamed. He knew it was a huge step for Josiah. He wanted to make sure Josiah knew how much he appreciated it.

Josiah trotted toward his clothes, and Kaspar looked away as he shifted back to his human form and dressed.

"They didn't tell you what they want from me?" Josiah asked.

Kaspar peeked, then turned around when he saw that Josiah was dressed. "Julian didn't say. It was a short text, and I have no idea what he was supposed to work on today, so I have no details for you."

Josiah nodded grimly. "I expected this to happen." He looked at Kaspar. "You weren't disgusted."

Kaspar frowned. "What should I have been disgusted by?"

"Me. My coyote form."

"I don't understand." Kaspar rose to his feet and brushed the earth that clung to his jeans where he'd knelt on them.

"I'm a coyote shifter," Josiah said. "We attacked the cete. We burned Thomas's house down. We almost hurt Kari and Calder, and we hurt other people."

Kaspar strode toward Josiah. He didn't touch him, but he made sure Josiah was looking at him. "Were you there? Did you plot the attack with your brother?"

Josiah shook his head, his eyes wide. "Of course not."

"Did you help them when they attacked? Did you set the house on fire?"

"I didn't do anything."

Kaspar grinned. "Exactly. Whatever happened, you had nothing to do with it. The fact that you're a coyote shifter doesn't change that. There are good and bad coyote shifters, just like there are good and bad bear shifters. I'm not disgusted by your coyote form, and I know no one here is." Kaspar frowned. "Is that why you haven't been shifting with us? Because you think we would be afraid of you or something like that?"

Josiah shrugged and looked away. "We hurt a lot of people."

"*You* didn't. Your father and your brother did. And they hurt you, too. You need to include yourself in that group."

"I don't want to remind people of what was done to them. It's enough that I can't live without the memories. I don't want people to hate me."

Kaspar's heart broke a little. "No one hates you. Some

people might not like you, but then, Calum doesn't like anyone but himself. But we know you're not your father or your brother, and that you had nothing to do with what they did." Kaspar suspected Josiah was at his limit with the conversation, so he gently knocked their shoulders together and tilted his chin toward the house. "Now, if we're done pouring our hearts out, we should get to the office. I don't know how long it will take for Julian to arrive, but I'm curious to find out what this is about."

Josiah finally smiled. "I didn't hear you pour your heart out. I did most of the talking."

"That's because I don't need to. I'm one of the lucky ones. And I have a boyfriend who listens to me whine."

Josiah laughed, and it was the best sound Kaspar had heard all day.

When Julian and the others arrived at the Bishop House, Kaspar and Josiah were already in the office. It was a relief, even though Julian wasn't looking forward to the conversation. He wouldn't want to be in Josiah's place, and he would do everything he could to support him.

Kaspar rose to his feet. He smiled at Julian and moved toward the door, but Josiah touched his wrist, and Kaspar turned back toward him. "Will you stay?" Josiah asked.

Kaspar looked at Julian, who nodded. He didn't have a problem with Kaspar staying. He would tell him what was about to happen anyway.

"He can stay," Calder agreed. "If it makes you more comfortable, it's not a problem."

They settled around the office, Thomas behind the desk with Calder leaning against it, Julian in the free chair on the other side, Kaspar standing behind him and Josiah. He had a hand on both their shoulders, and Julian relaxed.

It was weird how he'd already gotten used to Kaspar's presence in his life. Just having him there helped him feel better, and he could feel the stress drain out of his body. He still had something important to do, but he was home, and he knew he wouldn't go back to the council building until tomorrow. Once this meeting was over, he would be able to relax and be with Kaspar for a bit.

"Do you have any idea why we asked to talk to you?" Thomas asked.

Josiah looked over his shoulder at Kaspar. "I have a pretty good idea, yes. And my answer is no. I don't want to become the alpha."

Thomas grimaced. "I understand. We suspected that would be your answer."

"Yet, you still wanted to ask."

Calder sighed and crossed his arms over his chest. "We had to. If it weren't for the human team, we would give you more time. Hell, if it weren't for them, we wouldn't have asked you at all. But their leader talked to us today, and he wants us to find an alpha for the coyotes. He's not wrong."

"Did you tell him that the council doesn't have a say in who becomes the next alpha?"

"I did. But he pointed out that he and his team are here to keep the peace in the forest. He wants to be sure that the next coyote alpha is on the right side, and that won't happen if we let the coyotes choose someone."

Josiah shook his head. "You know this is impossible."

"If you could just think about it—"

Josiah got to his feet. "No. I don't need to think about it. I don't *want* to think about it. I never want to go back. The band were my abusers, all of them. No one tried to help me when my father and my brother hurt me. They looked the other way, and I'm doing exactly the same thing. I don't care if they never get another alpha, or if the band is disbanded, or whatever. Do what you want with them, but don't involve me. I'm done with them. As far as I'm concerned, I'm not a coyote shifter anymore."

Julian watched him stride to the door and leave. The door slammed behind him, making everyone in the room wince.

Kaspar sighed and sat in the chair Josiah had just left. "That could have gone better," he said.

Calder glared at him, but there was no heat in it. "We all expected that reaction from him."

"Yeah, well, do you blame him? After what the coyotes did to him, I don't. Did you know that I found him in his coyote form earlier today . . . when Julian told me to find him? He was terrified I might be disgusted with him because of what the coyotes did to the cete. He thought I was going to hurt him because I'd seen him in that form."

Julian's eyes widened. He'd noticed that Josiah kept to himself, especially when the other carriers shifted and played together in the forest. He hadn't thought much about it. He'd figured it was normal, considering everything Josiah had gone through, but he hadn't expected that was the reason behind it. "Did you tell him no one here cares?" he asked.

Kaspar nodded. "Of course I did. I wanted him to know that no one hates him for what he is. I told him that just like bear shifters can be either good or bad, or somewhere in the middle, the same goes for the coyotes. It's not his fault that his father and his brother were terrible alphas who only thought of themselves."

"We can't disband the band," Calder said. "Where would the coyotes go? No, we have to find an alpha, and I don't know who can take that role if Josiah doesn't want it."

Julian rubbed his forehead. He had a slight headache, and he knew it wouldn't get better until he rested. He wasn't used to being so mentally active, and he needed some time to get used to it, but instead, he'd gone ahead full steam, and he was right in the middle of things now. "I'll talk to him," he said. "I don't know how much good that will do, but I'll try. It won't be easy."

"As long as we try. Luther didn't give us a deadline, but he's going to want to know what's going on eventually. You heard him."

Julian had, and he knew they were lucky as it was. Other people would have demanded a name right away, or they would have tried to take things in hand even though they didn't know anything about shifters or how the forest worked. Instead, Luther was giving them space to do their thing, but they had to give him results. That was going to be almost impossible with Josiah so angry with the band.

Thomas rose from the chair. "Calder and I are going to head out."

Julian got to his feet, too. "I'll walk you to the door."

"Stay here," Thomas said with a smile. "We know the way, and that you're exhausted. How is it going with the council?"

Julian grimaced. He would rather not talk about it when he wasn't there, but Thomas was technically his alpha. "It's complicated. There are a lot of things to remember. And it feels like my brain is too small for all of it."

Thomas laughed. "You'll manage. If Calder did, so can you."

"Hey," Calder protested. "What's that supposed to mean?"

Thomas shook his head and headed to the door. "Nothing."

"That didn't sound like nothing," Calder said.

Julian listened to them as they bickered on their way to the front door. Their voices became softer as they moved away, and he turned toward Kaspar, who was still sitting in his chair.

Kaspar opened his arms, and Julian slipped into them, settling on his lap. He kept one foot on the floor, just in case he was too heavy.

"How are you feeling?" Kaspar asked. He raked his fingers through the hair on the back of Julian's neck, and Julian sighed in relief and happiness. He pressed his face against Kaspar's neck and closed his eyes, enjoying the moment. "I've felt better. I've also felt worse, though, so I guess that's a good thing."

"You don't have to go back to work today?"

"I should probably go over some files, but it can wait." Julian doubted he would be able to keep his eyes open as it was anyway.

He was tired, but he wanted some time with Kaspar even more.

Kaspar chuckled. "Why don't we go to your bedroom? We can get into bed and cuddle and talk about whatever you want."

Julian sighed. "You're too good to me."

"That's not true. Nothing is too good for you. You deserve all of this, and so much more."

And for the first time in what felt like a lifetime, Julian actually believed it.

Kaspar could tell this was weighing heavily on Julian's mind, so he guided him to his bedroom. He knew they'd been spending a lot of time there recently and that they had isolated themselves from the rest of the carriers, but he felt that Julian needed some time alone.

Even though he'd been living with the carriers for a while, Julian still wasn't used to the number of people he now had to deal with every day. He'd gone from only having his son in his life to having a wider group of people, to having pretty much the entire council building. That couldn't be easy, and it showed in how tired Julian looked.

"I should probably say hello to everyone," Julian mumbled to him as they made their way upstairs.

"They understand. We can come down for dinner and eat with everyone after you rest."

"I don't think Josiah will be up for cooking. Maybe I can put something together."

"Or maybe someone else can do it. You're not the cook, Julian. I know you like to take care of people, but right now, you have to take care of yourself." Or let Kaspar do it. He was more than happy to.

Julian's shoulders slumped. "You're right."

"Am I?" Kaspar teased him.

"I *am* tired, and someone else can cook. I worry about them, though, and about you."

"You don't have to worry about me. I'm fine, and I'm staying with you."

They walked into Julian's bedroom, and Kaspar closed the door. By the time it was locked, Julian was already sitting on the bed, but he wasn't doing anything, so Kaspar knelt next to him and took his shoes off.

"You don't have to do that," Julian murmured.

"I know. I'm doing it because I want to. I want to take care of you. You deserve it."

"I don't know. I didn't do anything for Josiah, and I want to help him so much. I just don't know how."

"His situation is difficult. There's no one else who can become the next alpha, but he doesn't want to, and it's understandable. I think you should give him some time to wrap his mind around it. Even though he already knew when you arrived, he needs some time. I don't know if he'll ever accept, but I'm pretty sure he *will* listen to you if you try talking to him in a few days. You can explain why you think it's a good idea, and we'll see what happens then."

Julian rubbed his face. "When did you get so smart?"

There was a hint of teasing in his voice, and Kaspar relaxed. "When I got with you. I have to be smart to keep up with you."

Julian shook his head. "You've always been smart."

Kaspar surged forward and pressed their lips together. Some days, it still felt like a miracle. Kaspar had never expected Julian to want him as much as he wanted Julian, yet here they were.

Kaspar pushed gently until Julian flopped onto his back. Julian wrapped his arms around Kaspar's neck, and they continued kissing, even though the position was slightly uncomfortable.

"We should probably get under the blankets," Kaspar murmured.

"I'm all for that." Julian hesitated. "I know we've only kissed since we got together."

"And it's perfect." Kaspar wouldn't care even if that was the only thing they did for the rest of their lives. As long as he had Julian in his life, he could make do with kissing and touching over clothes. He never wanted to push Julian, especially after what had happened to him.

Kaspar had no experience dealing with people who'd been traumatized. He'd seen it in several of the carriers, but he wasn't their boyfriend. He didn't want to hurt Julian in any way. He was terrified he would if he asked for more than kissing, though.

Julian bit his lower lip, and the gesture made him look younger. "I know. And I like kissing you, too. But I want more."

Kaspar froze. Those were the last words he'd expected to hear from Julian's mouth. "More?"

"I know I have exactly zero experience making love. The only time I, well, you know, I was forced."

Kaspar sat up. He hadn't thought about it that way, but

now, he was. "You're a virgin."

Julian sat up, too, and crossed his legs. "I'm not. I have a son."

"But you're a virgin. That time doesn't count because, like you said, you were forced. You were *raped*. That means you've never made love."

Julian hesitated, then nodded. "I guess that's right. I've never made love. I've never had someone love me and want me that way." He swallowed and looked away. "But I know you do."

"You're right." Kaspar wouldn't lie to him. "But me wanting you doesn't mean you have to do anything. I'll be more than happy to continue kissing you, even if we never do anything different."

Julian's fingers twined into the bottom of his t-shirt, and he rubbed the fabric with his fingertips. "What if I want more?"

"Then we can work up to it."

"What if I don't want to work up to it?" Julian looked at Kaspar. "I've had time to think about this. I never thought I would have a boyfriend and I would want to have sex with him, but I do. It's been almost twenty-six years since I was raped. I think I can do this."

Kaspar wanted to, but he was terrified he would hurt Julian. "Maybe you could, you know, fuck me?"

Julian wrinkled his nose, and it was adorable. "I want to do things the other way around. I can't get pregnant. We wouldn't have to ask anyone for condoms. I don't think I can survive the embarrassment. I almost died when Kari gave me a bottle of lube the other day."

Kaspar laughed. He was unsure whether or not Kari liked him, but he *loved* the guy right now. "So you have lube, but no condoms. We could do something else. There's no need to have penetrative sex."

Julian's expression twisted into a fierce determination. "I

want you to fuck me. Please. It's been so long since I started thinking about it. In the past twenty-six years, I've often wondered what it would feel like to have someone I love and who loves me do that to me. I've had endless days to think about it, and I want it to be with you. It's important to me. And like I said, I can't get pregnant, so that won't be a problem."

"I want it as much as you do, but I don't want to hurt you."

"You won't hurt me. I promise. It's been twenty-six years, Kaspar. It was a lifetime ago, and I swear I'll tell you if you do anything that hurts or makes me uncomfortable."

How was Kaspar supposed to say no to that? Julian was convinced and he was an adult. Kaspar wasn't about to try to change his mind, not when it was obvious that he'd already made it up. "All right. Why don't you get a shower? I'll be here when you come out."

Julian smiled. He jumped off the bed, and Kaspar laughed when he stumbled on one of his shoes.

They were doing this. Kaspar was nervous, but he was also looking forward to it.

He looked around the room. First, he had a few things to do.

Julian was nervous. He'd always known he'd be nervous the first time he had sex, even though he hadn't expected it to happen. He'd thought no one would want to have sex with him, not after what he'd been through. Yet here he was, with Kaspar waiting in the other room. They were about to have sex, and Julian had no idea what would happen.

He did know he would be cherished, though. More than most people, Kaspar could understand what had happened to Julian, and he would be careful. That was one of the reasons Julian wanted to do this with him.

The other reason was that he was in love with Kaspar.

The feeling had snuck up on him, and he hadn't fought it. He didn't want to. He might not have expected to feel like this about anyone, but he did, and he wasn't about to deny himself this. He didn't want to.

He looked at himself in the mirror and took a deep breath. He'd showered, and he'd taken extra care cleaning himself. He didn't know what Kaspar had in mind, but he wanted to be prepared.

He'd never felt less like he was, though. Of course, he doubted he'd ever feel entirely ready for this. He just had to take a deep breath — another one, then another one — and go out there, see what happened. Kaspar wouldn't force him into anything he didn't want and knowing that helped. Wanting Kaspar to fuck him also did.

But Julian was still hesitant.

He hadn't seen his naked body in more than two decades. He'd been avoiding his reflection since he'd arrived at Bishop House, but he couldn't anymore.

He was thin, thinner than he'd been when he was seventeen. He had stretch marks. His stomach was a little paunchy, and he knew he would never look like he had when he was seventeen again. He didn't want to, either. His body was proof that he'd survived. He'd gone through rape, a pregnancy, and a birth. He'd lived on his own, growing his food and not having electricity or running water, for more than twenty years. His body bore the marks, and it always would.

He hoped Kaspar wouldn't hate them. If he did, well, Julian would know what to do. He prayed he wouldn't have to, though. He hadn't expected this relationship, but he didn't want to lose it.

Wasting time in the bathroom wasn't helping. Julian had to take the next step, so he closed his eyes, turned toward the door, and reached for it. His hand hit the wood, and he had to open his eyes to find the handle. He chuckled at himself.

He was ridiculous, wasn't he? Whatever happened out there, he was at peace with himself. He'd lived through hell. He could withstand Kaspar not liking him the way he did, even though it would hurt.

He grabbed the handle and opened the door.

He blinked as he stepped into the bedroom. When he'd left it, it had been brightly illuminated and normal. Now, it was anything but.

Kaspar had drawn the curtains, and the lights were off. It was dimly lit, even with the rays of sunshine peeking from around the curtains. Kaspar had also found candles, and he'd placed them on the dresser. The bedsheets were drawn down, and Kaspar had even found the bottle of lube Kari had given Julian a few days ago. It was on the nightstand now, and Julian's cheeks heated at the thought of what he and Kaspar were about to do.

Kaspar was there, too. His hair was damp, and Julian suspected he'd showered in the bathroom he shared with his roommates. He was only wearing soft-looking pajama pants, and he was sitting on the edge of the mattress, his fingers linked, his knee bouncing as he waited. He jerked when he heard the bathroom door, and Julian smiled at him.

God, he loved Kaspar so much. He would have to tell him soon, but right now, he didn't want to break the moment. He wasn't sure how Kaspar would react to the words, and he needed to be sure first.

Kaspar's gaze raked over Julian's body. Julian hadn't taken clean clothes with him in the bathroom, so he was only wearing a towel around his waist. He had to resist the urge to cover himself, and he swallowed, waiting for whatever happened next.

Kaspar rose to his feet. He reached for Julian but stopped before touching him. "You're beautiful," he breathed, and at that moment, Julian believed him.

It didn't matter that he was old and that he would never have another child, that he had stretch marks and that his brown hair was turning gray. Kaspar thought he was beautiful, and it made Julian feel like he really was.

He swallowed. "You are, too."

Kaspar's cheeks and upper chest flushed. He rubbed the back of his neck and looked away. "I don't know about that."

Julian knew they could go one like this for a while. They both thought the other was gorgeous, but they didn't believe it of themselves, and that was okay. They'd get over it eventually, or maybe not. He had a hard time understanding how Kaspar didn't see himself as gorgeous, though. Julian wanted to count every single one of the freckles on Kaspar's face. He wanted to dig his fingers into Kaspar's thick auburn hair. He wanted to run his hands over Kaspar's wide shoulders.

Julian stepped closer to the bed — and to Kaspar. He reached for Kaspar, and Kaspar visibly relaxed, his shoulders going slack. He smiled, and it was easier for Julian to forget how self-conscious he was. Kaspar wasn't lying when he said he thought Julian was beautiful, and Julian believed him.

They kissed.

They were used to this. It was familiar by now, and it helped Julian relax even more, to the point that he barely realized it when Kaspar reached between them and unhooked the towel.

"Still sure about this?" Kaspar asked.

"Yes." Julian had never felt loved like this, and he didn't want it to end. He wanted to see this through and finally feel complete, like he wasn't missing a huge part of the life he should have had but had lost.

Kaspar gently guided Julian toward the bed. He didn't stop kissing him, and it was distracting, which Julian suspected was the point. Kaspar didn't want him to worry, but Julian wasn't, not beyond what would be normal for a couple's first time.

He'd had twenty-five years to deal with what his alpha had done to him. It hadn't been easy, and he didn't think he ever would be completely over it, but he was ready to leave it in the past, especially with Kaspar being his future.

Julian allowed Kaspar to lower him to the mattress. Kaspar didn't come with him, though. Instead, he stood over him and hooked his thumbs into the waistband of his pants.

Julian held his breath. He already knew he would love however Kaspar looked under his clothes. He didn't even care much, as long as Kaspar got on the bed with him. He loved Kaspar's heart and his mind, although he couldn't deny that Kaspar's body was a nice plus.

The pants slid down Kaspar's thighs. Julian licked his lips.

Kaspar's cock was already hard, and Julian couldn't help but stare. It curved slightly to the side, the tip a flushed pink. There was dark hair at its root, and hair also covered Kaspar's thighs and part of his stomach and chest.

He was perfect, and Julian needed him to come closer.

He opened his arms, relieved when Kaspar came. He crawled onto the bed, hovering above Julian as if he were afraid to hurt him if he laid on top of him. Julian wanted none of that, though. He grabbed the lube from the nightstand before he got too distracted and offered it to Kaspar, who looked at it like it was the first time he'd seen lube.

Julian couldn't help it—he laughed. "You can touch me. I won't break."

"I know. I'm just afraid to hurt you."

"I promise I'll tell you if you do." Julian raised himself on his elbows and kissed Kaspar's shoulder. "Please?"

That did it. Kaspar hesitated one more second, then he lowered himself next to Julian and grabbed the lube. He also kissed Julian, and Julian kissed him back, hooking an arm around his neck and pulling him close. He wanted Kaspar on top of him, but he knew that would come soon enough.

Kaspar was gentle and slow as he prepared Julian to take him. Julian had to school his breathing a few times because of the memories, but they were fairly easy to ignore once he focused on Kaspar. He was the one who was touching Julian, and he was doing it with a reverence and care that made Julian want to weep. He didn't, but it was a close thing.

Kaspar didn't ask Julian if what he was doing was okay, but Julian knew he kept an eye on him and that he would have stopped if Julian had given him any indication that he wasn't okay.

But Julian was, up to the point that Kaspar surprised him by grabbing his hips and pulling him on top of him.

Julian pushed away from Kaspar. "What are you doing?"

"I thought this would be easier for you. You won't feel boxed in, and you can set the pace and do what you feel up to."

Julian swallowed. When he'd imagined this, he hadn't thought he would be on top. "But you're still — I'm still — "

"We can change that, but I prepped you, so yes. You can sit on me."

"I've never done this."

Kaspar's smile was soft. "I know, and I'm looking forward to it. I want you to enjoy this, and I can see you're nervous. Maybe this will help you."

Julian doubted it, but he still sat on Kaspar's thighs. He looked down at him, wondering what was next. His stomach churned, but he couldn't deny he felt good knowing he was the one in charge. He wrapped his fingers around Kaspar's cock, smiled when Kaspar's hands landed on his hips, and he moaned and rose above Kaspar's cock.

It was tight and painful. It would have been too easy to allow the moment to pull him into the past, so Julian kept his eyes open and focused on Kaspar. Kaspar never moved to force him up or down or into a different position. He patiently waited until his cock was entirely inside Julian, then he gently pushed his hips up.

It was so entirely different from the time Julian had gotten pregnant with Kari. There was love in this, something he wouldn't have believed until recently. It still hurt a bit, but Julian's body was getting used to it, and once he started moving, it welcomed Kaspar inside him.

They moved together. It took them a few attempts to find the right rhythm, and it left a smile on Julian's lips.

He loved it. He loved *Kaspar*, and Kaspar loved him.

There was tenderness and care in every single one of Kaspar's movements, and Julian let it push him to orgasm. It had been a lifetime since he'd felt this much pleasure, and it was the first time he'd felt it with someone else. He screwed his eyes shut when he came, and he was relieved to find that he stayed in the present. It was easier not to forget that it was Kaspar moving inside him now, and Julian smiled when Kaspar's rhythm faltered. His cock pulsed inside Julian, telling Julian that he'd come, too.

Julian opened his eyes. Kaspar was staring at him, a frown on his face, and Julian smoothed his fingertips on Kaspar's forehead. "I'm fine," he said, his voice a croak.

Kaspar finally smiled. "Yeah?"

"Yeah." Julian hadn't felt this good in a long time, and he hoped it would never end.

CHAPTER SIX

Julian still hadn't spoken to Josiah, and it was time to do so. Whatever Josiah's answer would be, they needed to know so they could prepare. If Josiah refused to be the next alpha, Julian and the council would need to find someone else to take his place. As it was, Jacqueline was already making noises that her son would be the perfect alpha for the coyote band. If Julian had anything to say about it, he would never let either of them anywhere close to the alpha position, but he *didn't* have a say.

This was new territory for the council. They didn't usually select alphas, which meant that Jacqueline, being a coyote shifter, had more weight than they did in the decision. If Josiah didn't step up, it was entirely possible that they could find themselves in the hands of Jacqueline and her son, and Julian couldn't think of anything worse than that.

He knocked on Josiah's door and waited for him to answer. He knew Josiah was inside. He'd barely left his bedroom since the meeting with Thomas and Calder, and Julian hadn't pushed. He'd given Josiah a few days to think about it, even though he doubted it would change anything. They needed an answer, though. Luther hadn't asked again, but he would eventually, and Julian knew it would happen sooner rather than later.

He knocked again. "I'm not going anywhere until you open up," he said.

There was a moment of silence, then something moved inside the bedroom, and the door opened. Josiah glared at him.

"What do you want?"

"To talk to you."

"I already told you I don't want to be the band's alpha. I never want to go back there."

It wasn't anything Julian hadn't expected, but he'd come prepared. "Can we at least talk about why we want you as the next alpha?"

Josiah frowned. "It's because there's no one else."

"Actually, Jacqueline volunteered her son."

Josiah reared back. "Her son? He's as bad as she is. If you choose him, the band might as well die. That's what's going to happen. They're both just like my father and my brother. That's why my father chose her as the band's council member."

"We know. But no one else has stepped up, and since you, the rightful alpha, don't want the job, there's nothing we can do."

Josiah sighed heavily and opened the door wider. "Fine. Come in."

It was a step forward. A small one, but still.

Julian walked into the bedroom. There was a chair at the desk, and he chose to sit there while Josiah crawled onto the unmade bed. He wrapped the blanket around his body and stared at Julian from his nest of fabric. Julian didn't care. If that was what made Josiah feel better and safe, it was fine with him.

He swallowed. He didn't like this. He hated feeling like he was pushing Josiah to do something he didn't want and that would make him unhappy, but there really was no other way out of it. "Are you ready to listen to me?" he asked to be sure.

Josiah shrugged. "I don't think I'll ever be ready to listen to anything that has to do with the band, but I don't have a choice. Go ahead."

Julian wanted to tell him he *did* have a choice, but they both knew it would be a lie. "We talked. I mean, the council members on our side, the ones who passed the carriers laws. Having you as the next coyote alpha would help on several fronts. For one, you are your father's son and your brother's brother. It means that the coyotes would probably be fairly easy to convince you're the right choice since you share the same blood. The alpha position usually stays in a family, and that would be the case here."

"But I'm a carrier, and they all know it. They think I'm weak. They won't want me to order them around, especially after watching my father and my brother knock me around."

"They might not be happy about it, but once you're their alpha and you have the council's support, they won't have a say in it. We won't throw you into the middle of the band with no help, Josiah. If you accept, you will have a council team with you. They will be there to protect you and to make sure the coyotes stay in line. As long as you need them, as long as you don't have control over the band, they will be there for you. And the reason for that is that the council wants a carrier alpha."

Josiah wrinkled his nose. "There's never been a carrier alpha. I know Chris is supposed to be one, but his father isn't about to die or to step down. It'll be a while before he has to step up."

"You're right. There's never been a carrier alpha. That's why we want you to be the first one. If we had other options, we wouldn't ask you to do this. I personally think that you've already been through too much and that you should say no. But the council wants to take a step further now that we have the majority. We want you to be the first carrier alpha in the forest, and we'll support you in that." Julian paused. "There's also the council member thing."

"Jacqueline is the coyote council member."

"Because your father nominated her. But if you become the

alpha, you can nominate a new council member. That would give our majority even more weight. That's what we need now that we have humans looking at everything we do."

Josiah tightened the blankets around his shoulders. "So basically, if I say no, we're all fucked."

Julian could help but smile. "I wouldn't have said it like that, but it's a possibility. If you say no, I'm pretty sure that Jacqueline will push for her son to become the alpha. Since there is no one else, I doubt the band will say no or ask for someone else. That means that Jacqueline and her son will have control of the band, and while they won't have the majority on the council, she will still be a council member, and she'll make our life as hard as possible at every turn. Besides, the human team won't be happy if her son becomes the alpha. They want peace in the forest, just like us, and since they're sticking around, they'll be able to see that's not what we'll get with Jacqueline and her son."

"So I have to say yes."

Julian shook his head. "You don't. It would be the best outcome, but we won't force you. If you say no, then it's a no, and we'll never talk about it again. I promise. I represent you on the council, and I'll make sure that your rights and your will are respected. That's why I accepted this job."

Josiah cocked his head. "You didn't want it, though."

"I didn't. I thought that I would finally be able to live my life the way I wanted it. I was finally free."

"Yet you said yes."

"I felt it was my responsibility. I might not be over the moon happy about it, but it's the best thing for all of us. I represent the carriers, which means that I can protect you and everyone else. It might not be the life I expected for myself or the one I dreamed of, but it's a life I'm proud of. It's not an easy job, but someone has to do it, and since all of you had so much faith in me, I couldn't say no."

Josiah rubbed his face. "I'll think about it. That's all I can promise. I understand where you're coming from and what problems I'll create if I say no, but I can't say yes, not right now. I need to think hard about this. You know how abused I was, and I'm afraid that going back will push back my recovery. I'm fine physically, but not mentally, and I'm not sure I would be a good alpha. I don't want to say yes just because you expect and need me to. If I do agree, I want to be a better alpha than my father and my brother were. Since I can't promise that, I don't want to say yes."

He was taking this much more seriously than Julian had expected, and Julian was relieved. "Of course." He rose from his chair. "I'm afraid I can't give you more than a few days to think about it. Luther, the human leader, wants to meet you, and while he hasn't been pushing, it won't last forever. We really need to know what the next step will be and to plan accordingly."

"I'll let you know. I can't promise anything more."

Julian supposed it was better than nothing.

Kaspar was nervous, even though he shouldn't be. He already knew Morris wouldn't have a problem with him staying with the cete. This wasn't even necessary. He probably could have stayed with the cete without talking with Morris, but he felt he owed it to the alpha to tell him to his face that he wasn't coming back.

Which was why he was nervous. No matter how Morris reacted, he was still Kaspar's alpha. It was always slightly intimidating to talk to him.

"Do you want anything to drink?" Morris asked.

"No, thank you." It was strange to be back in sleuth territory. Kaspar had been allowed to move back and forth between the sleuth and the cete for a few weeks now, but he hadn't yet used that opportunity. He hadn't wanted to leave Julian and the other carriers alone, even though he didn't have to go through other territories. The cete and the sleuth bordered each other, and with the alliances between the two, Kaspar was still home.

But he hadn't been here in weeks. It didn't feel like his home anymore, and he wasn't quite sure why. He wasn't sure it mattered, either.

"What can I do for you?" Morris asked as he sat behind his desk. "Are you coming home?"

Kaspar sucked on his lower lip. "I'd like to stay with the cete."

Morris barely blinked. "I'm not surprised."

"You're not?"

Morris arched a brow. "If I expected you to come home, I would have mentioned something sooner. I was surprised to see you here today."

"I wanted to talk to you."

"That much is obvious. Just like it's obvious there's something between you and Julian and that he's the main reason you want to stay with the cete."

Kaspar wasn't ashamed to be so easily readable. "He's not the only reason, but you're right, he *is* the main one." Kaspar licked his lips. He wasn't used to talking about feelings, be it with Morris or anyone. The only person he did that with was Julian, and their relationship was still recent. Kaspar was used to keeping what he felt to himself, but right now, it looked like Morris wanted to know what was going on. "Julian and I are in love. We're together."

Morris beamed. "I'm happy for you both."

Kaspar had to ask. "Even though both of us are carriers?"

Morris leaned back in his chair and looked at Kaspar steadily. It made Kaspar want to wiggle, but he forced himself to stay as still as possible as he stared back at Morris.

"You already know some people are going to have a problem with your relationship," Morris said.

"I'm aware of that." Kaspar didn't care. Whoever thought that didn't matter to him.

"That said, I honestly don't give a shit. I want you to be happy, and if Julian makes that happen, that's more than good enough for me. I have never sold or bought a carrier, and I never planned to do it. It was never fair to keep you prisoner, and I'm glad that you're now free to be with whoever you want. The fact that both you and Julian are carriers doesn't matter. You're both human beings and men. *That* is what matters to me."

Kaspar had expected that answer, too, but he couldn't deny he was relieved at hearing the words coming out of Morris's lips. "Thank you."

"I want you to know that you're always welcome to visit or even to move back. I'm glad you found a family, though. I know your relationship with your parents has always been a little tense, and I'm sure that my behavior had a role in that. But I was trying to protect you. I wouldn't have kept you isolated otherwise. I realize now that it probably wasn't the best way to go about things, and I apologize."

Kaspar's eyes widened, and he shook his head. "I already know that, and you had no fault in this. It's true that my parents have always been a bit distant, but it was more because I'm a carrier than because of what you did. Just like you said, you kept me safe, and that's all that matters. I'm grateful for everything you did for me."

Morris smiled. "Don't start feeling guilty for leaving us behind. You're living your life, which is what we wanted when we decided to vote in carrier laws."

"It's just *strange*. The sleuth was my home and my family for twenty-five years. Then I moved in with the cete, and suddenly, my life was flipped upside down. Sometimes, it's hard to wrap my mind around it."

"A lot of things have changed lately. It looks to me like you're doing just fine, though. You have a boyfriend and a new home. I know you're close to most of the carriers who share the Bishop House with you. You should be proud of yourself."

"For what? I haven't done anything but hide."

"If I know you, Kaspar—and I like to think I do—you've done a lot more. Don't tell me you haven't been there for the other carriers. You're only twenty-five, but you're one of the oldest ones, right?"

"The third oldest now that Julian lives with us and Philip is leaving." It had been weird in the beginning, but Kaspar had gotten used to his role as a big brother of sorts.

"You've always been a caretaker, and I'm sure you take care of the carriers who need you. You found your place in life, and I'm happy for you. I'm happy to see that what we're working so hard for is bearing fruit."

Kaspar could never thank Morris and the other council members enough for the way they'd been fighting for the carriers. They had risked a lot, and Thomas had lost his house. But that hadn't stopped them. Kaspar felt like he owed it to them to live his life to the fullest now that he could.

He got to his feet. "That is all I had to tell you. I wanted to thank you for the opportunities you gave me, and the way you kept me safe. I feel guilty for leaving you and the sleuth behind."

"Don't be. You have nothing to feel guilty for."

Kaspar was starting to realize that.

He didn't know what the future held for him and Julian, but he *did* know they would be together, and that was all that mattered right now. He knew eventually he and Julian would have to find a house and that he would have to get a job. That would be tricky, since even though carriers were now free people and had the same rights as everyone else in the forest, it would take some time for people to get used to having them out in the open and trusting them. A lot of shifters might be in support of the carriers' laws, but even so, it was ingrained in them to see carriers as weaker and merely baby-makers. It wasn't offending to Kaspar, but it wouldn't help him find a job when he looked for one.

But that was a problem for another day. Right now, he had to head home. Home, where Julian was waiting for him. Home, something he'd never thought he'd have, not the way he did now.

CHAPTER SEVEN

Julian was stunned that Josiah had agreed to meet with the human team. He was surprised Josiah had agreed to leave the Bishop House, period. He was proud of Josiah, but he did wish this didn't have to happen.

Josiah hadn't been away from the Bishop House since he'd been brought there after being found in coyote territory. He'd been in bad shape, and while he'd healed physically, mentally, things hadn't changed. He was obviously terrified, even though he was doing his best to keep his chin high and look everyone in the eye. Jacqueline, the coyote council member, wasn't helping. She'd insisted on being here since she was a coyote shifter and their council member to boot, but Julian wished he could tell her to fuck off, and he wasn't one for swearing usually. That was how much she got on his nerves right now.

"The band hasn't approved this," Jacqueline said.

Julian didn't glare at her, but it was a close thing. "The band doesn't have to approve the human team meeting with anyone."

She glared at him so hard that he almost expected his hair to catch fire. She crossed her arms over her chest. "I won't take orders from him. I don't care whose son he is. He's a *carrier*." She put so much disgust and hate in the word that Julian didn't have to ask to know what she thought about carriers.

That probably included him. He didn't care. She could insult him as much as she wanted, as long as she left Josiah alone.

"So?" Kaspar asked. He was present because Josiah had wanted him there, and Julian was glad. It was slightly easier to face all these people with Kaspar behind him.

"Carriers cannot become alphas," Jacqueline answered. "It's obvious. There's a reason why our past two alphas did what they did to this — this — "

"Will you shut up?" Josiah snapped.

Julian blinked at him. He hadn't expected that, and he couldn't help but smile.

"My father and my brother were alphas before me, and the position has always been in my family. I'm the only logical choice," Josiah said. He looked Jacqueline in the eyes. "So yes, I may be the next alpha, and if you don't plan to obey my orders, then the only solution I'll have will be to kick you out of the band. Is that what you want, Jacqueline? Because it wouldn't be a problem for me."

Jacqueline's cheeks flushed, and she looked away. It looked like Josiah had managed to shut her up, which was a small miracle in itself. When she started bitching, she never seemed to stop. The problem was that whatever she was bitching about was usually something everyone else agreed on, like having a carrier becoming alpha. She wasn't a good person, and she'd shown it once again.

Julian and Kaspar exchanged a satisfied glance. Jacqueline wasn't totally tamed by any means, but for the time being, she was silent, and that was a good thing. Still, Julian needed to keep an eye on her, or maybe ask someone else to do it, since he had no idea where to start when it came to that kind of thing. He didn't doubt that Jacqueline would try something to get the upper hand again. She and her friends had the minority of the council, which meant they'd lost a lot of power. If Josiah became the next coyote alpha, she would lose even more. Even though Josiah and Julian hadn't talked about it in detail, Julian hoped that if Josiah became the alpha, he would ask Jacqueline to step down as a council member and nominate a new one. Choosing someone else would be hard, considering the options they would have, but at this point, Julian thought that anyone would be better than Jacqueline.

So yes, she would try something. From the way she behaved, he suspected she might attempt to contact Luther and tell him something was happening. Maybe Julian had too much faith in Luther, but it seemed to him that the human leader was a good person. A lot of people would have pushed for the coyotes to choose an alpha right now, without caring about who the alpha would be or how they would lead. They wouldn't have given them time to choose the right person and to make sure that the coyotes would be okay.

Some days Julian felt like the coyotes didn't deserve any of this, but they were still shifters. He could understand why they had never done anything to help Josiah. He'd seen the same thing happen with the weasels when he'd lived with them, and that was the main reason he wasn't planning to go back. Of course, Josiah hadn't spent almost thirty years of his life alone in the forest. Their situation wasn't the same, and Julian wanted him to heal sooner than he had.

There was a knock on the door, and Julian was relieved. He could see that Jacqueline wasn't done fighting, but he'd had enough of her for today. He was here for Josiah, and she was making it hard to focus on him.

A guard opened the door, and the human team walked in. Julian kept an eye on Jacqueline, and he didn't miss the way she looked at every single member as if trying to read them. That was probably exactly what she was doing. She wanted to know who was comfortable being in a room full of shifters and who wasn't. That would tell her exactly who might be susceptible to whatever she had to say. Luther certainly wasn't, but while he was the team leader, it didn't mean the others didn't have any influence on him. Things were getting complicated, and Julian wasn't sure what to do about it.

"Good morning," Luther said as he settled into one of the chairs on the other side of the long table. His gaze stopped on Josiah, and his eyebrows slightly rose on his forehead. "You're new," he said.

Julian blinked. There was no hostility in Luther's tone, thank God, but there was something else, and he couldn't quite put his finger on what it was.

Josiah's cheeks pinked. "I am. Do you know why you're here?"

This was surprising, too. Luther didn't seem offended that Josiah was talking to him that way, though. He chuckled. "I know." He looked at Julian and Calder. "You told me you wanted me to speak with the possible coyote alpha?"

Julian put a hand on Josiah's shoulder. "This is Josiah. His father and brother were alphas before him. We're trying to convince him to take their place now that they're gone."

Luther's gaze jumped from Josiah to Kaspar, who was standing behind him, but he didn't ask who Kaspar was. Apparently, he was only interested in Josiah. "So you're a coyote shifter."

"I am." There was pain in that statement, even though Luther might not understand why. Julian squeezed Josiah's shoulder, silently telling him that he was there for him. Josiah swallowed, then said, "Julian asked me if I would consider being the next alpha."

Luther leaned back in his chair. "And will you?"

Josiah looked away from him. "I *am* considering it. You might not be aware of it, but my father and my brother had conflicting relationships, both with each other and with me."

"They abused you."

Josiah's cheeks became even redder. "They did. They hurt me in ways no one should be hurt. That's the main reason I'm wary of taking their place. No one in the band helped me, and my first instinct is to let them rot."

"You won't do that."

"I won't?"

"You're here. You're talking to me about becoming the alpha. You didn't have to do that. If you're really planning to wash your hands of this, you would have stayed home instead of meeting with me. So no, you're not going to do it. I don't know if you'll accept, but you do know that this would be the best thing for everyone, so you'll at least consider it." Luther turned his attention back to Julian and Calder. "This is all I need for now. I'm sorry if you felt like I pushed you into making a decision. I understand how important alphas are for you, and I'm glad to see that you're working on a solution. I'll tell my bosses that."

Julian didn't slump in relief, but it was a close thing. Josiah had just earned them and himself a little more time to make the decision, which was what he needed.

Now Julian only had to pray that Josiah would be able to forgive what the band had done to him and make the decision to lead them.

Kaspar, Julian, Josiah, and Julian's alternate bodyguard were silent on their way home. Kaspar kind of wished Jacob had been with them, but he needed time off sometimes, and he'd stayed back at the Bishop House. Julian's other bodyguard, Diana, wasn't a bad person, but she was quiet. Instead of chatting like Jacob did, she watched everything with attentive eyes, and it was kind of awkward. She was good at her job, though, and Kaspar wasn't about to protest. Julian needed her.

The meeting could have gone much worse than it had. He wished Jacqueline hadn't been there, but they'd met her as they walked into the meeting room, and of course, she'd used the fact that she was the coyote council member to be at the meeting. She'd tried to raise hell, but Josiah had handled her surprisingly well. He had told her to shut up, and she'd obeyed. Julian was surprised, but he knew this wasn't over. What he'd seen before and during the meeting made it obvious that she was a crafty person who wouldn't stop for anything to get what she wanted.

She wasn't done with Josiah by any means, and Kaspar would have to keep an eye out for him, too. Of course, that would be impossible once Josiah went back to coyote territory — if he ever went back. He might still choose not to become the next alpha, although, from the way things were going, Kaspar doubted it. Still, it was a possibility, and after the meeting, Kaspar wasn't sure what he hoped for.

He wanted Josiah to be happy. He, more than almost anyone, deserved it. Being an alpha wouldn't make him happy. It would keep the peace in the forest, though, and Kaspar had to wonder what was more important — Josiah's happiness or peace. He knew which one he wanted to choose, but he also knew it might not be the right answer.

"We're going to need to have a meeting with the entire council," Julian said.

"After what happened with Jacqueline, I can't say I'm looking forward to it," Josiah answered.

"I don't think anyone looks forward to meeting with Jacqueline, but she has to be there. Until someone replaces her, she *is* the coyote council member, and there's nothing we can do about that."

Josiah sighed heavily. "I have no idea who to replace her with."

"Technically, it's not your job. Not yet. Not unless you choose to become the next coyote alpha."

Josiah looked tired, much more than Kaspar had ever seen him since he'd arrived at the Bishop House. "I don't know what to do. I don't want her to continue being the coyote council member or for her son to become the coyote alpha, but I also don't want to be the alpha. The situation is a mess, and I hate it."

Sometimes it was easy to forget how young Josiah was. They all were. Kaspar was only twenty-five, yet he was one of the oldest carriers in the Bishop House now that Philip was moving out. Besides Julian, only Turner was older, and he was twenty-six. Josiah was a few years younger, and becoming the alpha after everything that had happened to him would be hard. He would have support, of course, but still, it wouldn't be easy for him.

"You can always say no," Julian said quietly. "A part of me wants you to. I want you to be happy, and I know this won't do that, not in the short run."

Josiah leaned against the window. "But there could be a war in the forest if the wrong person becomes the next alpha. I know. Trust me. I've been thinking about this since you came to me the first time. I still have no answers for you. I wish I did, but I have conflicting feelings about it."

Kaspar was pretty sure they all did. It was good to see Josiah admit it, though.

Kaspar understood Josiah. He would never want to become an alpha, even if he had to. The thought of the responsibilities, of having so many people's lives in your hands, was terrifying, especially when those people had hurt you.

It would be so easy for Josiah to take the job and make the coyotes' lives hell. He wasn't that kind of man, but he was a man who had lost a lot and who'd seen people who should have had his back look away when he most needed them. Even if he agreed to be their alpha, it would take a lot of work for him not to lash out. It would take a lot of work for him to do just about anything if he accepted the job, and Kaspar was relieved he wasn't in his place. Still, he wanted to do more.

He just didn't know what.

Diana parked the car in front of the Bishop House, and Josiah hopped out as if his ass were on fire. He obviously couldn't wait to go back to his room and rest, forget about this alpha business for a while, and Kaspar didn't stop him.

The yelling did, though.

Josiah froze on the porch and looked at Julian and Kaspar. Two people were yelling at each other inside the house — from the sound of it, in the entrance — and it was obvious to all of them who it was.

Jacob and Chris were at it again.

Kaspar suspected it had to do with the other car in front of the house. He didn't recognize it, so he suspected it was an alpha's car. They were the only ones who were allowed to visit the Bishop House. Since Chris was involved in the yelling, it was probable that his father was here to pick him up and that Chris was yelling at Jacob for not fighting for him or something like that.

Julian opened the front door, and the yelling stopped. When Kaspar stepped inside, he almost laughed. Chris and Nico's father, Alpha Wiley, was in the corner of the room, his eyes wide as he stared at Chris and Jacob in the middle of the entrance yelling at each other. They both looked like they'd run a marathon with their flushed cheeks and panting, but Chris looked like he wasn't done yet.

He turned his attention back to Jacob, barely giving Kaspar and the others any attention. "I want you to fight for me," he told Jacob. "Is that so hard to understand?"

"You're leaving, Chris. What do you want me to do? Should I fight your father so you can stay here with me?"

Kaspar looked around. They could try to make a break for it and run for the stairs, but that would mean they would have to pass right between Jacob and Chris, and he doubted that was the best idea. Kaspar didn't want to end up in the middle of the fight if he could avoid it.

"Come with me," Chris yelled. There was desperation in his voice, as if he were about to lose everything. "I can't stay. You know I can't. But you can come with me."

Jacob shook his head. "I am *never* going to become an alpha mate. I'm sorry, Chris. I wish things were different. You know I do. But this is impossible."

"It's impossible only because *you* are making it impossible," Chris screamed. "I love you, you bastard. Don't you understand that? I would give up anything for you, yet you're not willing to do the same."

"Would you really give up anything for me? Because it doesn't look like it." Jacob rubbed his face. He looked tired and sad, and Kaspar wished he could help him and Chris. "You're not giving up anything for me, Chris. You're asking *me* to give up my entire life to come with you. You're going to go back to your life with your father and your brother, to your future position as the alpha. What am I supposed to do in the meantime? Even if I wanted to be an alpha mate, what do you expect me to do right now? It's going to be years before you take your father's position, and you'll be busy until then, studying and doing whatever alphas do. And me? Do you expect me to be a house husband or something like that? I have a job here, an important one. I protect Julian."

"Anyone can protect him."

"Maybe, but you can't expect me to go home with you and sit for the rest of my life while you go around doing alpha stuff. That's not me. *This* is me," Jacob said, gesturing at the room.

This was a disaster. Kaspar thought the two had talked, and maybe they had. But they were still fighting in front of everyone, yelling at each other and telling each other stuff they should have kept private.

Chris shook his head. "I don't want to leave you."

"It looks like you're going to have to. I'm not coming with you, Chris. I'm sorry." With that said, Jacob turned around and left.

Julian hated feeling this way, but he was relieved when Chris and Nico eventually left with their father. Alpha Wiley ushered them away, looking around as if he expected Jacob to come back and stop him.

Jacob didn't. Julian doubted he would change his mind. He'd sounded convinced of what he was saying and what he wanted. No matter how much Jacob and Chris loved each other, neither of them was ready to compromise, and without compromise, their relationship couldn't work.

Julian couldn't help but look at Kaspar, who was on the other side of the table. They were having dinner with the rest of the carriers and some of the guards, and Kaspar was saying something to Hector and laughing.

He and Kaspar hadn't had to compromise yet, but Julian knew it would come. They were lucky enough to live in the same place, and Kaspar didn't have a job. Neither of them was an alpha, so that wouldn't be a problem. They were both carriers, but hopefully, no one would care about their relationship. Even if someone had something to say about it, as long as they were in cete or sleuth territory, they would be safe.

This relationship was *everything* to Julian, and he was ready to do anything to keep it. He would even leave his job as a council member if he had to. He thought he could do some good by representing the carriers on the council, but he wouldn't do it if it meant losing Kaspar. He'd already given up so much of his life. He wasn't ready to do that again, not when he knew there were so many other people who could step into his shoes and take his place on the council.

"You're pensive," Josiah said. He was sitting next to Julian, and Julian had been surprised to see him there.

He'd thought for sure that Josiah would avoid him since he didn't want to become the next coyote alpha. Julian only wanted him to be happy, and if it meant that Josiah stayed away from the coyotes, that was fine with him. It would complicate things with the council and the humans, but Julian was convinced it was a problem they could resolve.

"I was thinking about Chris and Jacob."

Josiah grimaced. "I feel bad for them."

"So do I."

"It's not fair. I mean, I get why Jacob didn't want to go with Chris. I get why he doesn't want to be an alpha mate. But it's not fair that Chris wouldn't be allowed to step down, you know?"

Julian frowned. "Not allowed to step down? What are you talking about?"

Josiah shrugged. "I don't know. It sounds to me like Chris is going to be the next alpha because he has to, not because he wants to. It's what's expected of him. As long as he's been alive, his father has been telling him that he would be the next alpha. I don't know if he realizes there are other options."

Julian hadn't thought about that, but maybe he should have. Did Chris actually want to become the next bobcat alpha? Or was he doing it only because his father expected it from him? At this point, both were possible, and Julian wished Chris was still here so he could talk to him. "Do you think he would have stayed with Jacob if he'd been allowed?" he asked Josiah.

"I have no idea, but I think he would have at least given it a thought. As it is, he always said that he couldn't *not* go back home to follow in his father's footsteps. He thinks it's his duty, and while I understand where he's coming from, I don't think it's right. Why should he become the alpha if he doesn't want to?"

Why indeed. Julian had nothing to say to that. As much as he wanted to help Chris, he wasn't sure he could. Even if Chris didn't want to be the next bobcat alpha, Julian doubted he'd ever admit it. He was proud, and Josiah was right when he said that Chris had been groomed to take his father's place eventually. It would be hard to step away from that, even for Chris.

Julian was relieved when he and Kaspar were finally able to go upstairs. He was used to physical labor, but being a council member was a different kind of work. It made him even more tired, and he'd been feeling queasy for a few days. Maybe he'd caught the flu or something. He couldn't afford to be sick, though.

Now that they were away from the others, Kaspar seemed to be lost in his thoughts, and Julian left him in the bedroom while he went to the bathroom to shower.

Kaspar was still there when Julian came out of the bathroom. He was sitting in bed, his chest naked and the blankets bundled at his waist. He looked at Julian when he heard him come in and smiled, but it was a sad smile. "I hate what's happening between Chris and Jacob," he said.

"I was talking with Josiah about it. We agreed that it's a pity, but I don't think there's anything we can do."

"I don't know. I guess I hoped they would find a way to work things out. Chris deserves to be happy. He's young, but he knows what he wants, and he can finally have it, yet he and Jacob broke up."

"Not everyone can make it work. Sometimes love is not enough." Julian slipped into bed next to Kaspar and snuggled up against him.

He was still getting used to sharing a bed, but he loved it. He loved waking up in the middle of the night and turning to find Kaspar there, lightly snoring or mumbling in his sleep. He loved that in the morning, Kaspar was the first thing he saw when he opened his eyes, and in the evening, he was the last. Julian wanted this to last forever, and he thought he and Kaspar had a good chance to make that happen. They would need to talk and to compromise, but he was more than ready to do that.

"I wish I could do something for them," Kaspar said. He kissed the top of Julian's head.

Julian smiled. Yes, this was the rest of his life, and he couldn't wait to live it.

"What do you want?" Kaspar asked.

It took Julian a second to understand what he was talking about. "You mean for you and me?"

"Yes. It's obvious that Chris and Jacob want to be together, even though they haven't been able to make it work. Is that something you could want? Can you imagine yourself having a family with me?"

Julian frowned and sat up, but Kaspar didn't release him, so he stayed close. "I told you. I can't have children anymore."

Kaspar bit on his lower lip and looked away. "Maybe, but *I* can."

That was something Julian hadn't thought about. "You're right. You can." Julian had no idea what Kaspar was trying to tell him, but a mix of fear and excitement made his stomach churn. "Is that something you want? Children?"

Kaspar shrugged. He was still not looking at Julian. "I never really thought about it, you know? I always believed that eventually I would have to get married, because otherwise, the council would get their hands on me. I didn't think I would be with anyone for love." He looked at Julian. "But now I am. Because I love you, Julian."

Julian had to swallow because of how dry his mouth felt. "I love you too."

Kaspar's smile lit up the room. "That's good." He chuckled. "Of course it is. And I never thought I would have this.

That's why I didn't let myself think about having a family, a home, children. But since you and I got together, I've been wondering."

"You told me you weren't planning to get pregnant anytime soon," Julian pointed out.

"I wasn't. I wasn't sure how to handle it with your past. I didn't want to hurt you. I know you hate that you can't have more kids."

"But as you just pointed out, I can. I just wouldn't be the one carrying them." And while the thought was a strange one, it wasn't as bad as Julian had expected.

Only carriers and women could have children. This was what every other man felt like when he and their significant other decided to have children. They might not be able to carry the child, but it didn't mean they would love it less, or that they would be less of a father.

"Is that something you might want?" Kaspar asked. "Other children? Even if I'm the one carrying them?"

"Yes." Julian had never allowed himself to hope for a bigger family. He hadn't thought he could have one, and he hadn't wanted to hurt over it. But now, that was what Kaspar was offering him. "We can talk about it more, of course, but yes. I would be happy to have children with you."

Kaspar's smile widened. "I want to start trying."

Julian blinked. "Start trying?"

"Every time we have sex, I'm the one making love to you."

"Because I can't get pregnant, and that way, we don't have to use condoms." Both of them had been examined when they'd arrived at the Bishop House, and they were healthy — except for the fact that Julian couldn't have children.

"Right. But I want kids. You want kids. You don't have a problem with me carrying the kids, and I don't, either. Why should we wait? You've already waited long enough, don't you think?"

"You're only twenty-five." But the thought appealed to Julian.

"So? We might want three or four kids. Who knows?"

"We could wait."

"I don't *want* to wait, Julian. I'm ready."

He wanted children, and he wanted them with Kaspar. Why should they wait?

It was crazy. *They* were crazy, but Kaspar held his breath and waited for Julian to answer.

He knew he was only twenty-five. He knew he and Julian had only been together for a few weeks. But it felt right.

Kaspar had never thought he'd have this chance. Even though Morris had been a good alpha, he hadn't been able to work miracles. Kaspar would have had to choose someone to marry even though he didn't love them if Morris and the others hadn't fought for him to be free to choose. But now he was. He was almost twenty-six, and he didn't have to get married if he didn't want to.

But he kind of did. He didn't know what it was about Julian, but he could tell that they would be together forever. They worked well as a couple, and he knew they would work well as parents, too. Julian had done a good job with Kari, and he'd been alone. Even though it kind of terrified Kaspar to have children, there was no one else he'd rather have them with.

But he knew how Julian felt about not being able to carry a baby. He didn't want to take that away from Julian. He just wanted Julian to know that this was a possibility. He might not have thought about having children until recently, but he now did, and he wanted them with Julian.

"All right."

Kaspar blinked. "All right?"

Julian was smiling, and Kaspar found himself relaxing. "You want children. I want children. We want them together. People are going to think we're crazy, though."

"And we care about what they think?"

"Not really. I've never cared about what anyone thought, although that's probably because I've lived alone most of my life."

"Except for Kari. Do you think he'll be angry if we decide to have a child together?"

Julian shook his head. "He's been pushing me toward you ever since he realized I felt something for you."

"So he won't have anything to say? He won't even point out that it's too soon?"

Julian snorted. "Who is he to say anything? He and Calder weren't even together when he got pregnant."

Kaspar didn't know the story there, and he was curious, but he also realized it wasn't Julian's story to tell. He didn't know if Kari would ever tell him about it, but even if he didn't, it wouldn't matter.

Even though technically, Kaspar would be Kari's stepfather.

The thought made Kaspar shudder. He didn't want to be anyone's stepfather, but especially not Kari's, and not just because Kari was his age and could probably kill him with a well-placed glare. He wouldn't mind being a dad, though. He wanted it so much that it surprised him.

"So we're doing this?" It was hard to believe.

"I want to. There will never be a perfect moment for us to have a child. I don't think there's a perfect moment for *anyone* to have a child. But we have each other, and we're happy. We're free. We have a family. I'm sure Thomas won't mind if we ask him if we can move out of the Bishop House and into our own home. I have a job, and it pays well. You don't have a job yet, so it would be the perfect moment for you to have a child. Once they're old enough, you can look for something."

Kaspar smiled. "I thought you said it would never be a perfect moment? Because it sure sounds like it might be."

Julian narrowed his eyes. "You know what I mean. There's always a reason why we shouldn't have a kid. People are going to say that we don't know each other well yet, or that we're both carriers, or whatever. And they wouldn't be entirely wrong. But I know I love you, and I want to spend the rest of my life with you. Besides, I'm getting older. I might not be the one who will carry our child, but I'll still have a role in their creation, and the longer we wait, the older I'll get. I want another child while I can still enjoy them and be young with them."

"You're not old."

"Fine. I'm not old. But you can't deny I'm older. It's time for us to think about the future now that we have one. Don't you think?"

Kaspar wasn't sure how to answer, so he pulled Julian closer and kissed him.

They weren't usually frantic when they made love. Kaspar was always careful, because he knew that sometimes, no matter how much he denied it, the act reminded Julian of what had been done to him when he was younger. They'd only done this with Julian on the receiving end because Julian had insisted, but things would be different today. Kaspar didn't even know where to start, so he continued kissing Julian as he reached under the blankets and tried to push Julian's clothes away.

To his surprise, Julian rolled Kaspar onto his back. Kaspar's eyes were wide as he looked up at Julian, holding his breath.

"You're always the one in charge," Julian murmured.

"Only because you never said that you wanted to be."

"What if I do?"

Kaspar opened his arms. "I'm all yours, then. You don't even have to ask."

And he didn't. Julian had to look away from Kaspar to grab the lube from the nightstand, and Kaspar took advantage of it, pushing his pants down his legs under the blankets. When Julian noticed, he arched a brow, but he didn't say anything about it, and Kaspar grinned at him. He was impatient. So what?

He knew it would probably take more than once for him to get pregnant, but he was pretty sure Julian didn't mind practicing. *He* certainly didn't.

"You're eager tonight," Julian said.

"I'm always eager."

Julian chuckled. "That's true. And I can't say I'm any different. I love making love to you."

"Me too." Because it *was* making love.

Kaspar and Julian were in love, and they were about to build a family. Kaspar didn't know how long it would take for him to get pregnant, but he hoped it would be soon. He didn't want to wait now that he and Julian had made the decision.

He opened his legs and dropped his knees to the mattress as Julian settled between them. Julian was gentle. He always was. He made sure that Kaspar was comfortable with the entire process, staring at his face as he pushed his fingers inside him. It had been a while since Kaspar had touched himself there. He didn't need to, now that he had regular sex with Julian, but he missed it. He hoped they could continue to switch. They could get condoms after Kaspar had their kid.

But that would be in a while. In the meantime, Kaspar was going to enjoy feeling Julian inside him without a condom to separate them.

"Still sure you want a child?" Julian asked as he withdrew his fingers—Kaspar was pretty sure it was at least three—

from Kaspar's ass.

Kaspar nodded frantically. "I want your child. Fuck me, Julian. Make me yours and get me pregnant."

Julian's eyes widened and his pupils dilated. They hadn't used any kind of dirty talk in bed yet, but they were still exploring what Julian liked and disliked. Maybe this was one of the things he liked. Kaspar would have to try again eventually.

But not today. Today, he wanted Julian in his ass, and he wanted him there *yesterday*.

The head of Julian's cock poked at Kaspar's hole, and Kaspar hooked his legs around Julian's waist. He didn't try to push Julian inside his ass. Even though they'd already made love lots of times, this was still a first for Julian, and Kaspar wanted him to enjoy it.

Julian moved inside Kaspar just like he moved every single moment in his life — gently but sure of himself, quietly strong. Kaspar wouldn't have minded a bit more foreplay, but he doubted either of them would have the patience today.

It was strange to think that their lovemaking might result in Kaspar getting pregnant, but also exciting. Of course, sex with Julian was always exciting, and as he moved inside Kaspar, Kaspar closed his eyes and focused on holding the pleasure back for just a few moments.

All bets were off when Julian got a hand between them and wrapped it around Kaspar's cock.

Kaspar's eyes flew open, and he groaned when Julian jacked him off. He hadn't expected Julian to be this assertive in bed, but he *loved* it.

No doubt Julian realized how much Kaspar loved it when Kaspar came, yelling Julian's name. He didn't even care if the people in the rooms around theirs heard them. They already knew he and Julian were together, and while they would no doubt tease them, he didn't care.

If everything went right, if they were lucky, they were creating their baby, and Kaspar couldn't wait.

CHAPTER EIGHT

The baby bump was obvious now, and Kari was grumpy.
It made Julian want to smile, but he knew he'd better not.
Kari would get offended. It wasn't because of his pregnancy,
but rather because he was Kari. Julian loved him, but sometimes, he wished his son were easier to deal with.

Kari glared down at his stomach. He wasn't huge yet, but
he couldn't deny there was a baby in there now. "How much
bigger am I going to get?" he asked with a whine.

"You're not that big yet."

Kari glared at Julian, and Julian bit his lower lip. This *really*
wouldn't end well if Kari caught him smiling. "Not that big?"

"Come on, Kari. You're barely showing."

Kari pressed both his hands to his stomach. "Everyone
knows there's a baby in there."

"But not because you're showing. I mean, yes, you do have
a bit of a stomach, but if you wear loose clothes, no one is going to see it. You look fine. Happy." He made Julian envious,
but then he remembered that he and Kaspar were trying for a
baby, and he couldn't help but smile this time.

Kari's eyes narrowed, and Julian held his breath. He hoped
he wasn't about to fight with his son. There was nothing he
wanted less right now.

"What's making you smile?" Kari asked.

"Nothing. I can't smile when I'm with my son?"

Kari leaned over the table. "Of course you can, but this isn't
your usual smile. What's going on?"

Julian supposed he could tell Kari. He would have to

eventually, especially since he and Kaspar were hoping that if Kaspar wasn't already pregnant, he would be soon. "You know that Kaspar and I are together."

Kari flopped back into his chair and rolled his eyes. "Yes, Dad. I know you and Kaspar are together. You've been together almost since you moved to the Bishop House."

"That's not true."

"Right. You danced around each other for a while first. Sorry."

Julian bit his lower lip. He wasn't regretting trying to have a baby with Kaspar. He wanted it. But he knew some people would be against it, either because they hadn't known each other long or because they were both carriers. Not that it mattered since Julian couldn't get pregnant anymore. As it was, he was a normal shifter.

"Come on," Kari said. "What's going on? And don't tell me it's nothing, because I can tell when you lie."

"Kaspar and I are trying for a baby." The words were out before Julian could think too much about them. He knew if he did, he probably wouldn't say anything. He was terrified of what Kari's reaction would be.

Kari blinked. "Did I hear that right? I'm going to be a big brother?"

His reaction was better than Julian had expected. "Possibly. I don't know if Kaspar is pregnant yet. But we're trying."

Kari's smile was wicked. "I bet you are." He wiggled his eyebrows. "And I bet you have a lot of fun doing it, too."

Julian's cheeks heated, and he looked away. "I am *not* talking about my sex life with you." He knew he and Kari were close, maybe too much so. It was because he and Kari had spent so much time alone in the forest, and while Julian was happy to see that Kari had other people in his life now, he missed his son. He missed their relationship.

He knew that would change. They were settling down in a

more normal father and son relationship. It was still hard.

"Why Kaspar?" Kari asked.

It took Julian a second to understand what he was asking. "Estelle said I couldn't have more children." He hadn't told Kari because he didn't want Kari to feel guilty about it. It wasn't his fault that Julian had spent his entire pregnancy and had given birth to him on his own.

Kari grimaced. "I see. But you're still happy about this?"

"I'm over the moon. I might not be the one carrying the baby, but it doesn't mean I'm not their father."

"Exactly." Kari patted his stomach. "Trust me. If I could, I would transfer his pregnancy to Calder and have him carry the baby to term. Being pregnant is a hassle. People look at you differently, and you feel all kinds of weird."

The memories made Julian's stomach churn, and he pressed a hand against it. Of course, Kari noticed his movement and arched a brow. "Are you *sure* you can't have children?"

Julian shook his head. "It's just some heartburn. Nothing else. I suspect it's the job. It's quite stressful. I'm tired because of all the back and forth I've been doing between here and Northwood, and I'm always nervous when I have meetings. I'm still trying to find my bearings."

"You're doing a good job," Kari told him. "I'm proud of you, Dad. I didn't imagine this could happen, but I think it's exactly what you need in your life. You're still young. You need something to focus on that isn't feeling like an old man, or me."

Julian burst out laughing. "I just told you Kaspar and I are trying to have a baby. I'm pretty sure that makes me *not* old."

"I don't know. How old are you again? Forty-eight? Forty-nine?"

Julian glared and threw a bit of cookie at Kari's head. "You know damn well that I'm forty-two."

Kari laughed.

It was so good to see him like this, happy and relaxed. Julian had done his best with Kari with what he had when they'd been in the forest, but he'd always known it wasn't enough. Kari needed more people in his life. He needed a home with running water and everything else. He needed a family, and he had one now. Julian couldn't have been happier.

Well, maybe he could be, if Kaspar was pregnant. He wasn't sure how long it would take. He'd gotten pregnant after just once, but he knew that wasn't a normal situation. If anything, it was as far from being normal as possible.

But he and Kaspar were trying. And Kari was right—it *was* a lot of fun. Julian was discovering a part of himself that he hadn't thought was there, and he was in awe at himself and at how and what he allowed himself to do. It was awkward sometimes, and embarrassing, but he was working on feeling that way with Kaspar. He had nothing to be embarrassed about.

"Well, you were a great dad to me, and I know you'll be a great dad for your baby." Kari wrinkled his nose. "But I have to say it's going to be weird to have a kid almost at the same time. Think about it. My baby is going to be your baby's nephew. But yours is going to be younger."

Julian shook his head. "Does it matter?"

"Of course not." Kari hesitated. "I'm happy for you. I really am, and I hope you have everything you ever wanted with Kaspar. But you know you can come to me if anyone gives you any trouble, right?"

"I won't sic you on anyone. You're pregnant, and you've left that life behind. Haven't you?"

Kari shrugged. "I haven't killed anyone in a while, and I'm not sneaking around the forest. It doesn't mean I can't do it anymore if you need me to. I don't want people to bug you because both you and Kaspar are carriers."

"It doesn't matter. I might be a carrier, but I'm a barren one. People will realize that."

Kari didn't look convinced. "If you say so. Still. Remember that you always have me."

He was right. Kaspar was a carrier, and he was young. Some people were bound to think that what he and Julian were doing was wrong. Julian didn't care, but it might mean trouble. Luckily for Julian, he had a whole family supporting him now. He didn't have to fear what people would say anymore. He had Kari, of course, but also Calder, and Thomas, and the rest of the cete, and the sleuth. They would intervene if something happened.

That, more than anything, made Julian understand that he was making the right choices. He was living the life he'd always dreamed about but never thought he'd have.

Kaspar turned to the side and looked at his stomach in the mirror. He knew there was nothing to see, even if he was pregnant, but he couldn't help it.

He pressed a hand against it and wondered. What would he look like with a baby bump? Or when he was eight months pregnant? He could hardly imagine it, and it made him nervous. He hadn't changed his mind. He still wanted a baby with Julian. But now that the first emotions had passed, he couldn't help but wonder what would happen next.

Once he got pregnant, what would he and Julian do? Would they stay on at Bishop House, or would they ask Thomas if they could have a house in cete territory? Kaspar knew Julian would want to stay close to Kari and his grandson, and that was okay with him. He'd already spoken to Morris about it. He'd also mentioned it to Julian, but they should have a more in-depth conversation about it. They needed to talk about a lot of things.

A knock on the door made Kaspar jump. He pushed down his t-shirt and went to open the door.

Josiah looked at him, smiling nervously.

Kaspar couldn't help but wonder why he was here, and he waved him inside. "Come in. Is something wrong?"

Josiah chuckled. "I thought we were friends. Does something have to be wrong for me to come to talk to you?"

"Of course not." But Josiah had kept to himself since he'd arrived at the Bishop House, and even more after it had been suggested that he could be the next coyote alpha. Kaspar understood, even though he hadn't liked it. He was grateful to see Josiah was coming out of his shell. He hated the choice Josiah had to make, and he wished he could take it away from him, but he couldn't. The only thing he could do was to be there for Josiah and listen to him, like he would do today.

"What do you need to talk about?" he asked as he sat on the edge of his mattress. He was in his bedroom, the one he still officially shared with his two roommates. He hadn't moved his things into Julian's bedroom yet, even though he spent most of his time there.

"I don't know. I guess I just wanted to talk."

"About the alpha position?"

Josiah shrugged and sat at the chair by the desk. "The decision has already been made for me, hasn't it?"

"You can say no if you want."

"But if I say no, I'll be responsible for the destruction of the forest. Don't try to deny it. I know that's the case. If I say no, Jacqueline will push for her son to have the position. If he becomes the alpha, everyone is fucked. I wouldn't care about the coyotes' fate, but I do care about everyone else. Thomas gave me a home when I thought I didn't have one. He gave me friends and family, and even though sometimes I feel awkward, I know I won't lose them. I have to do this for him and for the cete, and for everyone else who sacrificed something to help the carriers."

Kaspar wished he could tell Josiah that no one else mattered but him, but they both knew it would be a lie. What Josiah wanted mattered, but did it matter more than the rest of the forest?

Even if Jacqueline's son became the alpha, Jacqueline wouldn't have the majority of the council. That was a good thing. What was bad was that apparently her son was dedicated to her. He would do whatever she ordered, and eventually, the coyotes would become a problem again. They might start a war, which was the last thing the forest wanted or needed.

So yes. Josiah didn't have the luxury of saying no. Kaspar hated that, but he could too easily imagine what would happen if Josiah didn't become the next coyote alpha.

He cleared his throat. "You know you won't be alone. You're stronger than you think, but even if you weren't, you would have help. Julian and I will always be there for you. You just have to call us. I know that Thomas and Morris will teach you how to be a good alpha. You know exactly what *not* to do. You saw what your father and your brother did, and you're not like them. You're a good man, Josiah. Possibly a better man than I am. You'll do the right thing."

Josiah hesitated. "I want to hurt them. The coyotes, I mean. They never tried to stop my father or my brother. I could have gotten killed, and they wouldn't have said anything."

"And it's a horrible thing. But have you tried putting yourself in their shoes?" That was a terrible thing to ask, but Kaspar wanted Josiah to understand where the coyotes were coming from.

Josiah was right, of course. No matter how terribly the coyotes had been treated or how scared they'd been, they still should have said something.

Josiah sighed. "I know. My father would have kicked their

asses if they tried anything, and they possibly would have ended up next to me chained to the wall. I thought about that. It doesn't make it easier to forgive them."

Kaspar was relieved. "No one said you had to forgive them."

Josiah snorted. "If I'm going to be their alpha, I *will* have to forgive them. I won't punish them for something they did long ago, especially not when it was self-preservation."

"But you can talk to them. Tell them how much it hurt. Tell them that you won't tolerate that kind of behavior anymore. Show them that you're not like your father and your brother. Earn their respect."

"I don't think it'll be possible. I'm a carrier. They're going to hate that I'm in charge."

Kaspar didn't miss the fact that Josiah spoke as if he'd already accepted the position. "But eventually, they'll realize how much better you are than your father and your brother. You'll show them through your behavior. The council will be there with you for as long as you need them to, and that means that you won't have to face the band alone. They might grumble and bitch and whatever, but you can do this, and Julian and I will be right there with you to make sure nothing happens to you."

"I don't think I can do this on my own."

"But you're not on your own." If there was one thing Kaspar was convinced of, it was that.

None of the carriers in the Bishop House would be alone again. Kaspar would make sure of that. Most of them had lost things. Some had been abused, raped, impregnated against their will. It would take them years to get over what had happened to them, if they ever could.

But they weren't alone anymore. Now they had an entire cete by their side, and each other, and Julian was fighting for them on the council. Julian would always have their best interest at heart.

"I never wanted to be alpha," Josiah murmured. "I don't know if I'll be any good at it."

"Even if you suck at it, you still won't be as bad your father and your brother, or as Jacqueline's son will be if he becomes the next alpha. Trust me. The band will realize that. They might not like you, and I have no doubt that they'll make sure you know that, but hopefully, most of them will realize that this is the best outcome for the band." And if they didn't, well, maybe they didn't deserve Josiah. Maybe they *did* deserve Jacqueline and her son, after all.

Kaspar knew it was petty to think that way, but he couldn't help it. He wanted the best for Josiah, and becoming alpha wasn't. But he suspected that Josiah had made his decision and that he would take his brother's place. He was too good, and he would get hurt. There was nothing Kaspar could do to help with that, but he would do his best to make sure that the band treated Josiah right.

He wasn't sure *how* he would do that, but he would find a way.

CHAPTER NINE

It had to be Jacqueline. It was the only thing that made sense. Julian looked at Josiah, who was walking next to him, his back ramrod straight. Someone had called a council meeting, and Josiah's name had been mentioned. Julian suspected that Jacqueline wanted to force the council to vote to choose the next coyote alpha. It was something that was only done when there was no heir, but in this case, there was one, so the vote would be useless.

Julian wasn't surprised that she was trying, though. He'd expected her to do so sooner, but he was glad she hadn't. It had given Josiah more time to get used to the idea that he would become the next coyote alpha. He hadn't accepted yet, but he was talking as if he had, so Julian was hopeful. Josiah wasn't happy about it, but he was doing the right thing, and that was what mattered.

"Are you sure I should be here?" Josiah asked.

"I don't see why not. The meeting is about you. I think you should be here."

"You can't be sure it's about me. You don't even know who called it."

"What are the odds? There's nothing as important right now than the next coyote alpha. Besides, I trust my sources." Mostly because it was Abel who had told Julian that Josiah had been mentioned. He wouldn't lie.

Abel wasn't a liar, which meant that Jacqueline was trying to overthrow Josiah as the next coyote alpha, and probably to push her son into the position.

She would have to walk over Julian's dead body first.

Calder was waiting for Julian and Josiah in front of the meeting room. He looked worried, but he waved at them when he noticed them. Julian made a beeline for him. "You know what's going on?" he asked.

"I probably know as much as you do."

"It's Jacqueline, isn't it?"

"I think she was the one to call the meeting, yes." He looked at Josiah. "This is your time to shine. Have you made your decision?"

Josiah glared at him, but there was no heat in it. "I haven't exactly been given a choice, have I?"

"You can still step away. We'll find a way around it."

Josiah shook his head. "There is no way around this. I'll do it. I have to. But you'd better not have been lying about the support the council will give me, because I have no idea where to start. It's not like my father ever taught me how to be an alpha."

Calder slapped Josiah's back. "Don't worry about that. We'll be with you every step of the way."

Julian was getting used to meetings, but he knew it could be intimidating, so he stuck close to Josiah as they walked into the room. Most of the council members were already there, and while a few ignored Julian and Josiah, most of them waved or smiled at them. They still had the majority, so whatever happened, Jacqueline wouldn't win. Still, Julian didn't like this. He didn't like that she felt so sure of herself that she'd called the council meeting. He was starting to wonder if she was hiding something, and he didn't like it. He didn't like being surprised, especially not by Jacqueline.

He guided Josiah toward the end of the table, where Abel was sitting. Julian left the seat between his and Abel's empty, and Josiah settled into it. He was bouncing his knee, and Julian let him be. It was normal for him to be nervous. Julian would have been surprised if he wasn't. Even *he* was nervous, and this had nothing to do with him.

The door slammed open, and Jacqueline strode in. She looked like she'd already won, and Julian made a face. She stood tall and was smiling, although Julian was satisfied when he saw her smile falter at the sight of Josiah sitting next to him.

"What is he doing here?" she asked, pointing her finger at Josiah.

Julian held his breath, but to his surprise, Josiah didn't look afraid. Instead, he crossed his arms over his chest and leaned back in his seat. "I'm not sure. You'd have to ask the person who called this meeting, since it's about me."

"*I* called the meeting. I didn't invite you."

"That's a pity. Julian invited me. I hope you don't mind."

Jacqueline's expression told Julian that she *did* mind — quite a bit. She snapped her mouth shut and glared at Julian, and Julian arched a brow at her.

She looked away and walked to the end of the table — the end opposite to where Julian and Josiah were sitting, of course — and looked around. "I called this meeting to hold a vote to choose the next coyote alpha," she declared.

"The council votes for alphas only when there are no heirs," Marjory, the bear council member, pointed out.

"There *are* no heirs, as the alpha's son died without children."

Marjory pointedly looked at Josiah, and Jacqueline huffed. "He's not the heir. He's a carrier. He can't become the alpha. He might as well be dead because of how useless he is."

That was a horrible thing to say, but Julian wasn't surprised Jacqueline had said it. He reached under the table and briefly squeezed Josiah's hand, smiling at him. Josiah nodded and turned his attention back to Jacqueline. "The last time I checked, I was still my father's son. Does it really matter if I'm a carrier?"

"Of course it matters," Jacqueline snapped. "Carriers can't be alphas. You're weak. You're only good to give an alpha children."

"Isn't that what some people think about women?"

Jacqueline's cheeks flushed. "How *dare* you?"

"You just told me that the only thing I have going for me is my ability to make babies. Doesn't the same go for you?"

"You little—"

Calder cleared his throat. "I think we should keep the name-calling outside council meetings." He looked at Jacqueline. "There is no cause for it in this meeting. Alpha Wilson has an heir, and he's right here."

"Carriers can't be alphas."

"Well, there's a first time for everything." Calder looked around the table. "But we can vote, of course. Anyone in favor of having Josiah take his brother's place as the coyote alpha?" he asked. He raised his hand as he did so, and Julian mirrored his position.

Most of the people around the table did. A few didn't, but like Julian had expected, they were in the minority. Jacqueline had forced a vote, and she'd lost it.

He wasn't sure why she'd thought she would win. Maybe because of the carrier thing, but things were changing in the forest. People were realizing that being a carrier didn't mean someone wasn't good enough, weak, or any of those things. That was why there were carrier laws in place now, and this was a huge first. Josiah would be a good alpha, even though he would need help in the beginning.

Julian would be more than happy to provide that help.

"How can you do this?" Jacqueline asked. "There has never been—"

"A carrier alpha in the forest," Marjory finished for her. "We are aware of that. You don't have to repeat it. And obviously, the majority here doesn't think it matters. You forced a vote, Jacqueline. You lost. You have to accept it."

Julian turned toward Josiah. "Congratulations, Alpha Wilson."

Josiah grimaced. "It's going to take a while to get used to that."

"But you'll get used to it. You'll be a good alpha."

Josiah wrinkled his nose, and to Julian's surprise, got to his feet. He looked around the table, his gaze stopping on Jacqueline. "Thank you for voting for me," he said. "Jacqueline?"

She glared at him. "You will *never* be my alpha. I won't allow this to happen."

"I guess you're free to move to another territory if that's what you want, or to Northwood. I'll be honest—I don't want you in the band, just as much as you don't want me as the alpha. You're free to go. Oh, and one more thing. You're fired."

Jacqueline's eyes widened. "Fired?"

"You're not the coyote council member anymore."

She laughed, sounding mean and evil. "I'm not the coyote council member anymore? Who will you replace me with? There's no one else."

"For now, I'll be the next council member. I can hold both roles for a bit, until I meet with the band and make a decision."

"That's unprecedented."

"So is having a carrier alpha. I want you out of band territory by the time I get there. I don't care where you go, but I never want to see you again."

Julian was so proud of Josiah that his chest felt like he was about to explode. He hadn't expected this, but he knew that he and the others had made the right decision. Josiah would be the perfect alpha for the coyotes.

Josiah started freaking out as soon as he stepped into the Bishop House. Julian had texted Kaspar to tell him what had happened at the council meeting, and Kaspar was waiting for them. He'd expected this to happen. Josiah was great at showing the others a good exterior, but Kaspar had known he would freak out.

The door slammed shut, and Josiah started pacing the entrance. "What was I thinking? Oh my God. I *wasn't* thinking, was I? I just accepted being the coyote alpha. I fired Jacqueline and told her to leave the band. What was I thinking?"

Kaspar wondered if they should let him continue to run his mouth and pace or if he should intervene. He looked at Julian, but Julian just shrugged.

"I don't have any kind of authority over the coyotes," Josiah continued. "They'll take one look at me and laugh their ass off, and probably run me out of the band. And how am I supposed to find a new council member? They're all dickheads."

Kaspar stepped in. He moved in front of Josiah, and when Josiah came toward him, he put his hands on his shoulders and forced him to look at him. "Breathe," he ordered.

Josiah shook his head. "I can't breathe. I can't do anything. Didn't you hear? I'm officially the new coyote alpha, and I fired Jacqueline. I also declared myself a council member. What am I going to do?"

Kaspar squeezed Josiah's shoulders. "The first thing is that you're going to breathe. Come on. Take a deep breath and let it out."

Kaspar watched Josiah as he finally obeyed. It took a few deep breaths for Josiah's shoulders to relax, but he finally managed, and Kaspar smiled at him. "You don't have to make these decisions alone. Remember that. It's overwhelming right now, but that's because the meeting just ended. Give yourself time, Josiah. Give yourself time, and lean on people who already told you that they were going to be there for you. You're not alone in this, even though you might feel like it."

Josiah shook his head. "I don't know. I should have said no."

"Maybe, but you said yes, and I know you. You won't back down."

"This is going to be a disaster."

"Maybe, maybe not. You can't know that until you try. Don't obsess over this right now. I don't think anyone asked you to do anything, did they?"

"No. Julian told me to take a few days to wrap my mind around everything. I don't think a few days will be enough, though."

Kaspar looked around, but to his surprise, Julian was gone. He frowned. It was strange for Julian to leave without saying anything, but especially so when Josiah was having a crisis. Whatever was happening, it had to be important, and Kaspar wanted to go to him and make sure everything was okay. He had to take care of Josiah first, though. He couldn't just dump him here.

"Why don't you go to your bedroom?" he suggested. "Get some rest. Think about what happened. We can talk later," he told Josiah.

Josiah rubbed his face. "Unless I run away, sure."

Kaspar chuckled. "You won't run away. I'm sorry, Alpha Wilson. But you agreed to this, and you're stuck now."

Josiah grimaced. "I need to see if it's possible to change my name. Alpha Wilson reminds me of my father and my brother, and that's not something I want to have to deal with every day for the rest of my life."

"I'm sure we can come up with something."

Josiah rubbed his face. "I know it's the least of my

problems. But there are so many of them. I don't even know where to start."

"You don't have to start anywhere, not right now. Take a nap. Watch TV. Read. Think about whatever you want that's not what's waiting for you. You won't have a choice but to think about it soon enough, so take the next few days not to, yeah?"

Josiah's shoulders slumped. "I guess. Thank you, Kaspar. I'm still wondering what the fuck I was thinking, but I'm not freaking out anymore."

Kaspar watched Josiah as he slowly walked up the stairs. He wished he could do more, but there was no other way for him to help. Josiah had accepted the role of the coyote alpha, and apparently, of the coyote council member. It was going to take some time for him to get used to it, but Kaspar would remind him as many times as he needed that he wasn't alone in this. Things wouldn't be easy, but they also wouldn't be as hard as Josiah seemed to think they would.

Or at least, Kaspar hoped they wouldn't.

He heard the door of Josiah's bedroom close, then looked around in search of Julian. Kaspar had no idea where he was, but he explored the downstairs rooms. He stopped when he heard someone throwing up in the bathroom. He wasn't sure it was Julian, but Julian was nowhere to be seen, and unless he'd left the house entirely, he had to be there.

Kaspar knocked on the door. "Julian?"

"Give me a second."

It *was* Julian puking in the bathroom. Kaspar frowned, wondering what was wrong with him. Julian had been especially stressed since he'd agreed to be the carrier council member, and while Kaspar had done his best to help him, he couldn't work miracles. There was nothing he could do against the meetings, the hours Julian spent working, and the stress. "Are you okay?"

The toilet flushed, and the door opened a few moments after that. Julian was pale, but when Kaspar reached for him, he shook his head. "I'm fine."

"That didn't sound like you were fine. It sounded like you were throwing up everything back to Christmas dinner."

Julian tried to smile, but it wasn't convincing. "I'm fine, I promise. I'm just overworked and not used to being around all these people. You know that. It's why I'm stressed, but I'm sure I'll get over it eventually. I'll have to, won't I?"

"Maybe I should call Estelle."

Julian grimaced. "No offense to her, but I'd rather not see her."

"She's the cete's healer. You're going to have to see her eventually." Especially if he continued throwing up. Kaspar hoped he was right and that it was just stress, but he doubted that was the case.

"Considering how our last meeting went, I'd rather not." He reached for Kaspar and took his hand. "I'm fine. I promise. It's just stress," he repeated as if that would be enough for both of them to believe it. He looked around. "Where's Josiah?"

"He went to his bedroom. I told him to get some rest, and the same goes for you. Why don't we go to our bedroom? You can get into bed and have a nap."

"I have too much work to do."

"And it can all wait until you rest. Come on. Overworking yourself to the point in which you're throwing up won't help anyone, least of all you and Josiah."

It took a few more moments to convince Julian to go upstairs, but Kaspar finally managed. He guided Julian to his bedroom, still wondering what was going on. He knew Julian hadn't been feeling well for a while, and while he'd allowed Julian to brush him off until now, he wasn't sure he could anymore. It hadn't been as bad as it was now, but something was seriously wrong, and Kaspar was going to have to find a way around Julian's stubbornness. He wasn't sure he could, but he needed to. He couldn't lose Julian, not now that he finally had him and they were planning to have a family together.

Julian was worried, but he hoped Kaspar hadn't noticed. He'd been feeling weird for a while, but he didn't want to see Estelle. He didn't want her poking at him. He wasn't used to it, and the first—and last—time they'd met, she'd had bad news for him. If he was sick, if something was happening to him, he didn't want to know yet. It was probably stupid to bury his head in the sand, but he couldn't help it. He had other things to focus on, and they took precedence. He already knew Kari and Kaspar would yell at him when they found out, but right now, it didn't matter.

"Are you sure you don't want to see the healer?" Kaspar asked as they climbed the stairs.

Julian shook his head. "There's no need to call Estelle. I'm fine. Just tired." And he was. He'd been feeling overly tired for several weeks, but he'd put it on his new job and the back and forth between the cete and the council building. Maybe it was more than that, though. He'd never been so tired that he had thrown up, and he wasn't sure that was why he'd been sick, but eventually, he would have to find out.

He allowed Kaspar to steer him into their bedroom. They hadn't moved in together officially, but it was a given that Kaspar would spend the night with Julian. Julian let Kaspar help him sit on the bed and take his shoes off, then his jeans. It felt incredibly vulnerable, and Julian wouldn't have allowed anyone but Kaspar to do this for him.

But he trusted Kaspar. He trusted him with his heart and with his life. Kaspar wouldn't betray him.

He was worried, though. That much was obvious in the way he was frowning as Julian slid under the blankets. Julian should probably get up. He had things to do. He already knew Kaspar would allow none of that, though. He might even call Estelle, and that was the last thing Julian wanted. He did *not* want more bad news from her.

So he pressed his head against the pillow and closed his eyes.

He wasn't surprised to hear Kaspar undress and slip under the blankets next to him. He rolled to his side and snuggled against Kaspar, smiling when Kaspar's arms wrapped around him.

He prayed he wasn't sick. He wanted this to continue. He'd just found happiness and was finally beginning to live a life he'd wanted for decades. It wouldn't be fair for life to take it away.

But then, life wasn't fair, was it?

Kaspar kissed Julian's forehead. "Are you sure you're okay?" he asked in a whisper.

"I'm tired." And Julian was, so much so.

"Being tired doesn't make you throw up. I'm worried, Julian."

Julian kissed Kaspar's naked shoulder. "You don't have to be worried. I promise I'm fine."

He knew Kaspar wasn't convinced. There was nothing else he could tell him, though.

"If you're sick again, we're calling the healer," Kaspar said. His voice was uncompromising, and Julian had to say yes.

He didn't want to, but he wasn't stupid enough not to realize that if things got worse, he *would* have to see Estelle. "I promise. I'll call her if I feel sick."

"I wish you would see her now."

"I will if things get worse." Julian didn't want to talk about it again, though. He didn't want to *think* about it.

It was too easy to obsess over the fact that he might be sick and that he could lose everything he was working for soon. He didn't know what it could be. He'd spent twenty-five years alone in the forest. He hadn't seen a healer for all that time, and God only knew what it had done to his body. He'd been lucky until now, but it looked like his luck might have come to an end, and he wasn't ready to deal with that.

"How did the meeting go?" Kaspar asked.

Julian was grateful for the change in topic. "Good. Well, unless you ask Josiah. He'll tell you it was a disaster."

"He said he's both the coyote alpha and the coyote council member?"

"He fired Jacqueline in front of everyone. You should have seen it. I was so damn proud of him."

"I can imagine. How did he end up being the council member, though?"

"Jacqueline pointed out that he would need to appoint a new council member to replace her. I'm pretty sure he panicked and decided it was going to be him because he couldn't think of anyone else. And I get it. He hasn't had the best relationship with the band, and he's probably not sure who should take Jacqueline's place, not when the band ignored his abuse for so long when they could have intervened. The new council member needs to be a good person, which right now doesn't seem to be available, at least not in the band."

"He's going to overwork. He needs to focus on being the alpha, not a council member."

"I know. I'll do everything I can to help him. There was no other choice, though. Jacqueline was making a fuss about him being a carrier and therefore not being allowed to be an alpha."

"And I imagine that some of the council members were on her side."

"They were. But they were the minority, even more so now

that Jacqueline isn't in the picture anymore."

"Will she *stay* out of the picture, though?"

They both knew the answer to that, and it was *no*. Jacqueline wasn't going to roll over and let Josiah do what he wanted. She was going to fight. She was used to holding a place of privilege. She'd been the coyote council member for years, and she enjoyed the authority and the power over people she considered inferior to her. She would find a way to get back at Josiah, and that scared Julian. She was ruthless, much more than Josiah was. Julian couldn't even begin to imagine what she would do, but he knew Josiah would be defenseless from it.

Kaspar kissed his forehead again. "We'll take care of him."

"I know. I'm still worried." Julian had to remember that Josiah wasn't alone anymore, just like he wasn't.

"Maybe we can talk to Thomas and see if he will give Josiah a bodyguard like he did with you."

"The council should probably do that. They promised him a team to keep him safe and to help him once he went back to the band."

Jasper sighed. "I'm not looking forward to that. I'm going to miss him."

"So will I, but he's starting a new chapter in his life. He needs all the support he can get."

"And he'll have it."

Everything was changing, wasn't it? Josiah would eventually leave to become the coyote alpha. Chris and Nico were already gone. Kari was living with Calder, and he was going to have a baby. Julian was the carrier council member, something he had never thought could happen.

And Kaspar. Julian hadn't seen that coming, either, and he was glad he hadn't resisted. The age difference didn't matter anymore, and it probably never had. It had been a way for Julian to keep himself safe and separated from Kaspar and the others, but not anymore. This was where he belonged. He wanted to protect the carriers and to be with Kaspar.

And whatever illness he had, it was threatening that. He wasn't sure what he would do once he couldn't avoid talking to Estelle anymore, but he didn't like how easy it was for him to imagine the worst. Maybe it was because before, the worst thing that could happen always happened. Julian knew how Josiah felt. No one had ever raised a finger to help him when he was still a boy and his alpha, one of the people who should have protected him, had raped him and gotten him pregnant. He knew no one would have helped if he'd stayed and given birth to Kari. His life would have been hell, and he might have been one of the carriers who were rescued recently.

Or he might have been dead. He was forty-two. He doubted his alpha would have wanted him for this long, especially if he'd managed to get him pregnant more than once. He would have discarded Julian, and the thought made Julian shiver.

Kaspar's arms tightened around him. "Everything okay?"

Julian had to breathe through the memories that hadn't happened. It was so easy for him to imagine that they might as well have. "I'm fine." He really wasn't, but what could he say? There was nothing Kaspar, or anyone else for that matter, could do or say to make this better.

Julian's life had gone the best way it could have considering the circumstances. He needed to remember that instead of thinking about things that *could* have happened.

He was safe. He was happy. There was no way for him to know how long that would last, so he should make the most of it while he had it.

CHAPTER TEN

Julian was in the living room going over some documents when he heard the front door open. He leaned back against the couch, trying to see who it was. The house was quiet, which was a small miracle. Everyone seemed to be either in their bedrooms or outside in the forest playing around in their animal form. Julian was jealous. He wanted to shift and play around, too, but he was working, and that took precedence. Maybe if he was quick enough, he could still join the others when he was done.

Seamus waddled in. The sight made Julian smile. It reminded him of when he'd been pregnant with Kari, and he got to his feet to welcome him. "What are you doing here?" he asked.

Seamus jerked, then grimaced. "I didn't hear you arrive."

"Sorry. Didn't mean to surprise you. Are you okay?" Because he didn't *look* okay. He was grimacing and holding a hand to his back. Of course, that was normal. With how big his stomach was, he probably needed help for balance. Julian wasn't convinced that was what was happening, though.

Seamus shrugged. "I've been better."

Julian frowned and gently steered Seamus toward the couch. "Sit down. You shouldn't spend too much time on your feet. What are you doing here? Do you need to see someone?"

Seamus shook his head. "I just needed to get away from the house for a bit. The walls were closing in on me."

That was something Julian could understand. "Cabin

fever?"

"That, and Alex is going crazy. You'd think I was about to give birth by the way he's been behaving."

Julian sat next to him. "How long do you still have?"

"Estelle says a month." He grimaced. "I'll be honest. I kind of want this to be over. I liked being pregnant in the beginning, but I'm done with it now."

Julian laughed. "I remember that all too well. You still have a month, though."

Seamus rubbed his stomach. "I know. I want her to be okay, so I don't want her to rush, but still. I hate running around and not being able to see my feet." He wrinkled his nose. "And my dick. It's getting hard to go to the bathroom."

Julian chuckled. "That's what you have Alex for, isn't it?"

"Nope. That is one thing I don't want Alex to help me with. I know he loves me, but that's one step too far." He sighed. "I'm sorry. I shouldn't talk to you about this stuff. It's private and whatever. I know. But I don't want Alex to help me in that situation. It's already bad enough that he has to put my shoes on for me."

"I'm sure he doesn't care." If anything, he was probably more than happy to do it and much more for Seamus.

"I know. That doesn't mean I want him to do it."

"He makes things easier for you, though. That's a good thing."

Seamus grimaced. "I'm sorry. I'm grateful for everything he does, even though it doesn't sound like it. And I shouldn't whine. I don't have a reason to."

"Don't worry about it. I might have had Kari a while ago, but I still remember how it was. You have every right to whine. You're growing a baby inside you."

"Are you sure? Because you don't look like you're okay. I'm really sorry I was an ass. Your situation was so much worse than mine, and I'm ready to bet you didn't whine."

"I'm fine. I promise." Actually, Julian wasn't fine. He was still feeling queasy, and he still hadn't seen Estelle. Kaspar would have his ass if he didn't make an appointment, and not in a good way, but it was easier for Julian just to push it back and promise he would go eventually.

Seamus grimaced again and rubbed his back. He had to lean forward to do that, but it was hard in his condition.

Julian supported him, then helped him rub his back. It might be a too-intimate gesture, but he remembered all too well what the end of his pregnancy had been like, and he wished Seamus didn't feel so bad. "What's going on?" he asked.

Seamus shrugged. "Nothing. It's just my back. Estelle warned me that it would hurt, with all the weight I'm carrying in my front, but I didn't think it would be this bad."

Julian frowned. "Your back hurts."

"Yes. It's been hurting badly since last night."

"And nothing you've done helped?" That didn't sound good, or rather, it sounded like Seamus might be in labor.

"Nothing. Alex gave me a massage, and I took a bath, but it still hurts. That's one of the reasons I wanted to leave the house. I need to focus on something that's not the pain."

"That's the only thing you're feeling?"

Seamus shrugged. "My entire body hurts, but then I guess that's what being pregnant is about."

Julian didn't want to alarm Seamus, but if he really was in labor, they needed to get him to Estelle, and fast. He'd been having contractions since last night, and he hadn't realized what was happening. He might be close to having Scarlet, and while Julian had given birth to Kari on his own, he didn't want to risk Seamus's life or his daughter's, not when Estelle was close by.

He cleared his throat. "I don't want you to panic," he started.

Seamus's eyes widened. "If you say that, it's a guarantee I *am* going to panic. Just spill the beans, Julian."

"I think you might be in labor."

Seamus shook his head. "It's not possible. She still has a month to go."

"Some babies come sooner than expected. It shouldn't be a problem, but we need to get you to Estelle."

Seamus was pale now. "All right. Are you sure I'm in labor?"

"Not a hundred percent, but then, I'm not a healer. But the fact that your back has been aching since last night might mean that you're about to give birth. It sounds like you've been having contractions for a while. I'd rather be safe than sorry."

"Of course." Seamus tried to get to his feet and grimaced. "You're going to have to help me."

"Stay here. I'm going to grab Kaspar, and we'll take you to the alpha's house." It was almost finished, and Alex and Seamus had moved in with Thomas and his wife. It was a tradition for the alpha heir to live with his father. One day, the house would belong to Alex and Seamus, but in the meantime, they would share.

Julian didn't want to leave Seamus alone, but he needed to. He took his phone out of his pocket as he headed toward the kitchen. "Estelle?" he asked when she answered.

"Julian? Is something wrong?"

"I'm at the Bishop House with Seamus. I think he might be in labor."

"In labor?"

"I know Scarlet isn't due for another month, but yeah. From what he says, it's a possibility."

"Of course it is. Do you need me to come there?"

"I told him we'd take him home. Alex will want to be there."

"Do you need help?"

"We can manage. I'm getting Kaspar." Jacob, too. Neither Kaspar nor Julian could drive, and they would be focused on Seamus anyway. "We'll be there as soon as possible."

"Good. I'll be there, too. Just time enough to grab my stuff and head out." She hesitated. "Julian?"

"Yes?"

"How is he doing?"

"He's in pain, and scared. He's okay, though."

"Good. Tell him that it doesn't have to be a bad thing. Some babies just want to come early, and I'll do everything I can to make sure his daughter is okay. Him, too."

"Of course." Everyone would do what they could to make sure Scarlet was okay. She was the next alpha's daughter, and eventually, she might become the alpha herself. It would be a first, but then, lately, there had been a lot of firsts in the forest.

But of course, they needed to make sure that Scarlet came into this world safe and sound first, and Julian would do everything he could to make that happen.

Kaspar was relieved when they finally got Seamus home. He was obviously in pain, and Kaspar was freaking out. He didn't have any experience with this kind of stuff, but he supposed he should get used to it if he was going to have children of his own.

Right now, he might be about to change his mind. He'd known that giving birth would hurt, but what Seamus was going through was awful. He was trying to keep up a good front, but Kaspar didn't miss how he jerked every so often and how he clutched his stomach and his back.

Jacob parked in front of the new alpha's house and ushered them out of the car. Kaspar and Julian helped Seamus walk, even though Seamus tried to wave them away. Julian knew what he was doing, and Kaspar was going to follow his lead rather than Seamus's, who had no idea what was happening except that he was in pain.

"I can walk on my own," Seamus whined.

"I know you can. It doesn't mean you should have to," Julian pointed out. "Come on. We're almost there."

The door swung open as they reached the top of the porch steps. Estelle stood there, alongside Patrick, a coyote shifter who'd moved in with the badgers and was learning how to be a healer.

"What are you doing?" Estelle asked Seamus.

"Nothing."

"It looks like your little girl is in a rush to come into this world."

"Is there anything you can do to keep her inside?"

Estelle shook her head. "I'm sorry. I doubt it. I'm going to check, of course, but from what Julian told me, you're about to give birth."

She and Patrick stepped closer and took charge of Seamus. Kaspar watched him toddle, and he couldn't help but wonder how he would be when he would see him again. He knew labor could be very long, but apparently Seamus had started last night already. Maybe it wouldn't be that long after all.

The sound of two cars arriving made all of them look back. Kaspar frowned when he didn't recognize the cars, and he frowned even more deeply when he saw the human team climb out of them. This was not the right moment for them to do whatever they were about to do. Not only was Seamus in labor, but Kaspar also wasn't feeling well. He might throw up in their faces, although from his point of view, it wouldn't be a bad thing.

"What's going on?" Julian asked, stepping between Seamus and the humans.

Kaspar didn't remember all their names, but he did

remember the name of the leader, Luther. He came to stand in front of Julian, his expression uncompromising. "We got an anonymous tip that the badgers and the bears were plotting something," he said.

Kaspar barely resisted the urge to roll his eyes. Anonymous tip. *Right.*

Julian crossed his arms over his chest. "What are you talking about? We're not plotting anything."

"We need to make sure."

"And how are you going to do that?"

"We need to talk to all of you."

He gestured at the rest of his team, and they deployed. They disappeared around the house, and Kaspar knew they were surrounded.

What the fuck was happening? It was too easy to realize who had given the anonymous tip, but Kaspar didn't care. Luther and the rest of his people didn't know Jacqueline as well as everyone in the forest, did, and they wouldn't know that she was lying. Still, even if they'd had an anonymous tip from someone else, why were they behaving like this.? They were already viewing the badgers as enemies, which was what their anonymous source had been trying to do.

"We aren't doing anything we shouldn't do," Julian said. "I can call Thomas for you if you want, but he'll tell you the same thing."

"We're going to search the house."

"You have no right."

Luther arched a brow. "Are you sure about that? Because as far as I remember, I have every right to do whatever I want in the forest."

Kaspar grimaced. This wouldn't end well. He had no idea what to do, but he wanted to help. He knew it would be better for him to stay away, though. He really might puke in Luther's face, and he was pretty sure things would get worse if he did.

One of the humans was standing behind Luther, and he looked so satisfied that Kaspar couldn't help but wonder if he had something to do with this. Probably. Jacqueline was good at manipulating people, and she apparently was doing it again.

"We're going inside," Estelle said. There was a hint of hesitation in her voice, but Julian nodded without looking at her.

"We'll be right behind you," he said.

"You're not going anywhere," Luther said. He gestured toward Estelle and Patrick. "Stop them."

The guy behind him took a step closer, and Kaspar went ramrod straight. Seamus needed to be taken inside, and he needed to go now. They couldn't afford to waste time because the humans were stubborn and thought they were enemies.

He stepped closer to Julian, offering a united front to protect Seamus. Luther blinked, but he didn't say anything. His man tried to step around them, and Kaspar placed himself in front of him. He might be a carrier, but that didn't mean he was weak. He was taller than the human, and possibly stronger. If things came to that, he could shift and defend Seamus until everyone else arrived.

Thomas was on his way. Kaspar knew that. Alex was with him, and they would arrive soon. Kaspar and Julian needed to protect Seamus for only a few minutes.

Kaspar hoped they could. He wasn't sure what would happen if the humans did something and it hurt Seamus. It would be a disaster, and that was the last thing they needed. The humans were here to stay, and they had to learn to live with them. It looked like they were the first who didn't want to try, though.

The man in front of Kaspar bared his teeth. "Step aside," he snapped.

Kaspar shook his head. "Leave him alone." There was so

much disdain in the man's voice that told Kaspar exactly what the guy thought about him.

Kaspar didn't care. He wouldn't move, not until he was sure Seamus was safe.

"I can kick your ass, badger. I won't hesitate to do it if you continue blocking my way."

Kaspar was terrified. He knew how easily he could get hurt. He knew how easily Julian and Seamus could get hurt, and the thought made his stomach churn. He wasn't used to this kind of situation. He wasn't armed, even though he could be in a few seconds by shifting. His claws would be good to defend the others, but the guy in front of him had a gun, and he no doubt knew how to use it. If he shot at Kaspar, Kaspar might die.

What would happen then?

This was a fucking disaster, and Julian wasn't sure what to do. The only thing he knew for sure was that he had to keep the humans away from Seamus until Alex and Thomas arrived, though, so he stayed right where he was, even though he felt like throwing up in Luther's face. He was grateful for Kaspar's presence, but he was terrified Kaspar would get hurt if he didn't move. He had no idea what to do, and he was panicking.

"Stop them," Luther said. "Before something happens. I don't want anyone to get hurt, but you have to see that there is a better way around this. Just stop and allow us to look through the house."

This was it. Julian was *not* moving, no matter how scared he was. "Can't you see he's in labor?" he snapped. "He *needs* to go inside. He has to get to his bedroom before something happens to the baby. And if it does, it will be *your* fault. I hope you're ready to deal with that."

Luther took a step back. "I'm sorry?"

Julian gestured toward Seamus, who looked terrified and was clutching his stomach while Estelle and Patrick held him up. "In labor. Can't you see it? He's about to have a baby."

"What the fuck?" the man in front of Kaspar said.

"He needs to go inside," Julian repeated. "Please." He softened his tone. He didn't want to fight with Luther. He hadn't yet changed his mind that Luther was a good person. He wasn't acting like one right now, but that was because he'd been lied to, and he probably felt betrayed after he'd been promised that the shifters in the forest wanted nothing more than to live their lives.

"He's a man," Luther said.

Julian rolled his eyes. "Yes. I can see that. So?"

"Men don't have babies."

"Well, unless he ate a basketball, he *is* about to have a baby, and he needs to go inside. Or do you want him to give birth here?"

"It has to be a trick," the man in front of Kaspar said. He tried to walk around Kaspar, but Kaspar didn't let him.

Julian could have cried when he heard the car. Thomas was driving, and he and Alex threw themselves out of it as soon as it was parked. Thomas looked like he was about to start bashing heads together, and Alex barely even looked at the humans as he rushed toward Seamus.

Julian relaxed. He'd protected Seamus until Alex and Thomas had arrived, and now, he didn't have to anymore. He could relax. He could give in to the fear that gripped his guts.

His stomach churned, and he looked around. He wouldn't make it inside to the bathroom, so he ran toward the bushes next to the house and leaned over them, throwing up everything he'd eaten all day. He heaved and closed his eyes, wondering what the fuck was happening.

He'd been throwing up too often for it to be normal. He'd

tried to pass it off as stress and being tired, but he could tell there was something else, and he was terrified to find out what it was. What if it was cancer? Or something just as lethal? He and Kaspar were trying to have a baby, and Kaspar might be pregnant already. What would Kaspar do if Julian died and left him alone?

"Julian?"

Julian jerked, and his stomach churned again. He threw up some more, holding himself up against the house until he was sure there was nothing else to throw up in his stomach. A warm hand rubbed his back, and he knew it was Kaspar. He wanted to tell him that he was sorry, that he was grateful for his presence, but he wasn't sure he could without crying.

He needed to find out what was happening, but now wasn't the moment. Things weren't over yet. Seamus might be with Alex, but the humans were still here, and the problem was still unsolved. Everything might still blow up, and Julian needed to make sure that wouldn't happen.

He straightened and cleaned his mouth with his sleeve. "I'm fine."

Kaspar wrinkled his nose. "You don't look fine to me."

"I promise I'm okay. Is Seamus inside?"

"Yeah. Alex, Estelle, and Patrick whisked him away as soon as Thomas took over. You don't have to worry about him anymore."

Julian relaxed. He rubbed his face and wished he could brush his teeth, but the best thing he could do was chew some gum, so he took a piece out of his pocket and threw it in his mouth. "I need to hear what's happening between Thomas and Luther."

"You need to go inside and rest. This isn't normal, Julian. You've been throwing up too frequently."

That was exactly what Julian was worried about. "I'm fine. I promise." He stepped away from Kaspar. He had to. He couldn't allow Kaspar to distract him, not with something this important happening.

He walked toward Thomas and Luther. They were staring at each other, and Thomas had made it obvious that he wouldn't move. The guy Luther was with looked like he wanted to strangle Thomas, but luckily for everyone, he didn't even move toward him.

"What's going on?" Thomas asked.

"Like I told your friend here, we got an anonymous tip that the badgers and the bears were planning something."

"Planning something? Anonymous tip? And you thought it was a good idea to barge into my territory and try to stop my son-in-law from having a baby? What were you trying to do? Hurt him?"

Luther rubbed the back of his neck. "To be honest, we weren't aware of the fact that shifter men could have children."

"That doesn't sound like a good excuse. Would you have stopped a pregnant woman?"

"Of course not, but again—"

Thomas shook his head. "Enough. I don't care what you thought or didn't know. I want to know what's happening."

Julian held his breath. He understood why Thomas was annoyed and angry, but he hoped he wouldn't make Luther even angrier than he already was. He didn't know what they would do if the human team decided to attack. Seamus was inside right now, giving birth, and he needed to be protected.

There was nothing Julian could do, though.

"I want an explanation," Thomas said. "Now. I know that you're the representative of the humans, but I don't care. This is my home, and you barged into it without hesitation. I want to know why."

Julian held his breath. This could go either well, or terribly wrong, and he had no idea which way it would tilt. He was pretty sure that if there was still something in his stomach, he would be throwing up right about now.

Something was very wrong with Julian, and Kaspar was worried. He could tell that Julian wouldn't budge until this was resolved, though, so he did his best not to show it. He didn't want to seem weak to the humans. He didn't think it mattered, but just in case, he wanted to make sure they were showing a united front and that they weren't distracted.

"We got an anonymous tip."

Thomas looked like he might punch Luther. "You already said that. I want more information. Who got the tip? What did the caller say? Was it a man or a woman? Why did you believe them rather than me?"

Luther gestured at the man who was still staring at the door as if he expected Seamus to come back. "Randy got the phone call."

Thomas arched a brow. "A *phone call*? Does he have the phone number of a lot of shifters who live here? Because I assume your anonymous call came from a shifter in the forest."

"I didn't give anyone my phone number," Randy snapped. "They called me."

"That's exactly what I was saying. How did they get your number? You're new here, and with the way you're looking at me, I doubt you view shifters in a good light. I can't see you handing out your phone number to people you don't know, and who you think aren't worthy of breathing the same air as you."

Randy opened his mouth, but Luther shook his head at him, and he snapped it shut. Luther turned to Thomas again. "I don't think that how the caller got Randy's number matters right now. What does matter is that this person told him that the badgers are planning to break out of the forest and take it over."

Thomas blinked. "I'm sorry, but I don't think I understand. Are we trying to break out of the forest, or to take it over?"

Luther frowned and looked at Randy. "Randy?"

Kaspar wasn't surprised when Randy looked away instead of answering.

"Which one is it?" Thomas asked. "Either we're trying to break out, or we're trying to take over," Thomas pointed out. "It looks to me like you acted impulsively instead of thinking about what was told to Randy—if it was even told to him in the first place."

"Are you saying I lied?" Randy asked.

Luther's eyes narrowed, and he raised a hand. It was enough to silence Randy. "We had to check."

"You're welcome to, of course, but you won't find anything. We're almost done rebuilding, as you can see." Thomas gestured toward the house. He and his family lived here already, but it was obvious it still needed a coat of paint and a few more things. "My family and I are settling down again. I'm about to have a granddaughter. I don't have the time or the will to take over the forest, or worse, to break out of it. Why would I want to do that?"

"To take over the human world," Randy snapped.

Thomas looked at him like he was stupid, and Kaspar shared that opinion. "Take over the human world? Again, *why* would I want to do that? I have everything I want or need in the forest. I have a home, a family, and as much space as I can want. Why would I want to take over the human world? And more importantly, *how* would I do that? Even if you put together all the shifters in the forest, our numbers are nowhere near close to those of the humans. Even if we did break out, it would take no time at all for the humans to find out and kick our asses back into the forest." Thomas shook his head. "I'm sorry, but whoever called you was lying."

"You can't know that," Randy said.

Kaspar was starting to be bothered by Randy. He seemed to have a problem with them, and Kaspar didn't know what that problem was. He didn't care, either. He just wanted Randy to leave them alone.

"Randy," Luther said. His tone told Randy and everyone else everything he needed to know. Even Kaspar was able to read it, and he wasn't the greatest at that. If Randy continued flapping his mouth, he would pay for it.

Randy snapped his mouth shut and glared. Kaspar grinned at him. He liked Randy much better now that he was silent.

"You're welcome to look around cete territory," Thomas said. "If you could stay away from the house for now, though, I would be grateful. As you know, my son-in-law is having a baby right now, and I need him to stay calm and focused."

"That's not possible," Randy said.

Luther looked like he might be about to throttle him. "Randy," he repeated.

Thomas ignored Randy. "You need to knock on doors instead of barging in, though. Even though you were sent by the humans and we have no say about your presence here, this is still our home. You have no right to walk around the way you've been doing. If you believed your anonymous caller, you should have come to me, not barged into my home like you were doing."

"I apologize," Luther said.

Randy made a strangled sound. Kaspar wondered if he was about to leave or do something just as stupid. He looked like the kind of person who might.

"I accept your apology," Thomas said with a nod. He looked back at the house, and Kaspar knew he wanted to go in and check in on Seamus. He wanted to do the same, and he and Seamus weren't even related.

"Thank you. And you're right. I acted impulsively. I should have thought better about what was happening, but it was easier to just act." He looked at Randy. "Randy? We need to talk."

Things wouldn't end well for Randy. Kaspar could tell just by the look in Luther's eyes. Luther had realized that something was wrong, and he was about to find out exactly what. Kaspar would be curious to find out, even though it wasn't his business. He was still one of the people threatened by the humans, and he wanted to know what was happening, especially when it came to that anonymous source. It felt like someone was working against shifters from the inside — that was the only thing that made sense — and it couldn't be good.

Chapter Eleven

Randy was in trouble, and Julian was happy about it. He didn't care if it made him petty or a bad person. He could tell that something was up with Randy, and he was curious to find out what it was.

He already knew Jacqueline was behind this. It was obvious. Josiah had fired her from her council member position, and she wanted revenge. Julian wasn't surprised about that, but he *was* surprised that she was using the humans to get it.

"Randy? How did that person get your phone number?" Luther asked.

"How should I know? I got a phone call, that's it."

"Did you know anyone in the forest before we got here?"

"Of course not. How would I know anyone here?"

"Well, it's obvious that someone has your phone number, and I want to know how and whom."

Randy shook his head. "Why does it matter? We have a reason to arrest all of those animals. Who cares who the anonymous tipper is? She gave us the weapon we needed, and we can use it and go home."

Julian jerked back. He'd suspected that at least a few people on the human team thought shifters were barely more than animals, but it was still hurtful to hear it. Julian didn't want to be friends with any of the humans, but that didn't mean he enjoyed anyone telling him that he was only as good as his weasel was.

"I don't want to hear that from you ever again," Luther snapped.

"You saw them! That guy is having a *baby*. You can't tell me that's normal."

"I don't care what's normal and what's not. I want to know what happened, and I want to know *now*."

"I told you, I don't know how she got my phone number."

"She? That's the second time you've said *she*."

"The woman who called me. She asked me if I wanted to help her."

"Help her do what?"

"Get rid of the shifters in the forest."

"And you said yes."

"Of course I did. That's why we're here. Besides, it's not like they're human beings."

Luther sighed and gestured. Julian wasn't surprised to see several team members come closer. He *was* surprised to hear Luther say, "Arrest him."

"What are you doing?" Randy protested.

"You're under arrest. I'm sending you back home."

"You can't do that. I didn't do anything wrong."

"You almost started a war. That's very wrong." Luther turned toward Thomas. "I apologize. I should've known better than to listen to Randy. I thought I could trust him."

"I understand. He's a member of your team, and if you can't trust them, who can you trust?" Thomas asked.

"Exactly. Still. I shouldn't have acted instinctively the way I did. I should have listened to you."

"You should have. But as long as you look into what's happening, I'm happy with the outcome. I want to know who called your man and got him to do this."

Thomas had to suspect it was Jacqueline, but he didn't say anything. If she had tried to start a war, the shifters would deal with her. It wasn't the humans' business.

Luther nodded. He turned to watch his team members drag Randy to one of the cars, then turned back to Thomas and hesitated. "Is he going to be okay?"

Thomas frowned. "Who?"

"Your son-in-law?"

Thomas smiled. "He will be. He's just having a baby."

"I can lend you my medic if you want."

Thomas shook his head. "We have a healer."

"If you're sure."

"I am. I know it's surprising to you, but here in the forest, we're used to men having babies. Seamus will be fine. Well, not right away, but eventually. Feel free to call me if you need anything."

"I will. I promise I'll find out what happened. I won't tolerate what Randy did, and I'll get to the bottom of the situation."

"That's all I'm asking for."

Julian was relieved. He'd thought things would end badly, but instead, the only one who was in trouble was Randy. It could have gone so much worse.

The thought made his stomach churn. He didn't puke again, but it was a close thing. Instead, he leaned against Kaspar, and Kaspar wrapped an arm around him, pulling him close.

Julian didn't miss the way Luther looked at them, but thankfully, he didn't say anything. Julian wasn't in the mood to defend his relationship with Kaspar. He wasn't in the mood to give the humans any more information than they'd already gotten. Even though Luther was trying to make things better, it didn't change the fact that he'd acted without thinking and that he shouldn't have. He wouldn't have if he'd been working with humans. The only reason he had, in this case, was that he was dealing with shifters.

But that was his job, wasn't it? He was here to police the shifters, and he'd believed his man. It was surprising that he'd allowed Thomas to reason with him, and that he was taking this seriously. Julian hadn't expected it, and he wasn't sure what to think of Luther anymore.

It didn't matter, because Luther was leaving — for now. Julian, Kaspar, and Thomas watched as the humans climbed into their cars and drove away. Julian only relaxed when the cars disappeared at the end of the driveaway. He hoped he wouldn't see any of those people anytime soon, but he knew better. He was the carrier council member, after all.

"Thank you," Thomas said.

Julian shook his head. "You have nothing to thank us for."

"You protected Seamus."

"Of course we did." What else did he expect them to do?

Thomas smiled. "I suppose I shouldn't be surprised. Why don't we go in? Estelle can tell us what's happening and how long it will be. And thank you for bringing Seamus home. He didn't tell Alex he wasn't feeling well, which is why Alex and I left."

"He mentioned that. He didn't realize he was in labor until I told him."

"Well, he was lucky to have you there." Thomas patted Julian's shoulder. "Let's go inside."

Julian followed, relieved that he would finally be able to sit down. He still wasn't feeling well, and he didn't want to think about what it meant.

Not yet. Eventually, but not yet.

Kaspar was relieved when they finally went inside. He wished this mess hadn't marred the moment, but at least things had ended better than he'd thought they would. Luther seemed to be a good man, just like Julian had said. Kaspar was surprised, although he supposed he shouldn't be.

It wasn't like he'd ever met humans. They lived outside the forest, where they belonged. They stayed away. They'd locked the shifters inside the forest, and shifters had to stay here. Kaspar didn't mind. The forest was his home, and it always would be. He didn't want to meet the people who lived outside, especially if he thought about the way they treated them.

But he had to admit that he was happily surprised at Luther's behavior, although he could have done without all the drama.

He *wasn't* surprised at Randy's behavior, though. There were bigots and assholes in every species.

"Thank you for bringing Seamus home," Thomas said. It had to be the tenth time he'd repeated that, and it made Kaspar smile. Scarlet wouldn't be Thomas's first grandchild, but technically, she would one day be the alpha, and that meant a lot. Besides, Kaspar suspected Thomas would be emotional with every single one of his grandkids. He was just that kind of man.

"Don't worry about it," Julian said. He was still a little pale, and Kaspar wondered if he should grab Estelle after Seamus had given birth and ask her to check on Julian. He wasn't sure he wanted to know if something was wrong, but he also *did* want to know. It was a horrible dilemma, but it was one they would have to face eventually. Today might not be the best day for that to happen, but with the way Julian had been denying something was wrong, it might be a good thing to be in the same house as Estelle.

They walked into the kitchen, and Kaspar blinked at finding Estelle there, filling one of those reusable bottles of water with a straw that kept water cold.

"What are you doing here?" Kaspar asked. "Shouldn't you be with Seamus?"

Estelle chuckled. "It's going to be a while. He doesn't need me there holding his hand, not when he already has Alex and Hope with him. Patrick is there, too. That boy needs to learn how to do this, so he's keeping an eye on things."

Kaspar was slightly worried that the only healer with Seamus right now was an apprentice, but he didn't say anything. Estelle knew what she was doing after all, and he certainly didn't.

"How is he?" Julian asked.

"Pretty good. He's dilatating, but like I said, it's still going to be a while."

The thought of what was happening in Seamus's pants made Kaspar feel queasy. He eyed the kitchen sink, wondering if it would be a good place to puke. Probably not since there were so many people in the room with them.

He swallowed. Estelle was still talking about how Seamus was doing, and Kaspar tried to ignore her. He was nauseous, and he suspected he might be pregnant. He didn't dare hope, though. "Do you have some time?" he asked Estelle before he could think better about it.

She blinked and looked at him. "Of course. Do you need something?"

"I'm not feeling well."

Estelle cocked her head and looked him up and down. "Of course. I can see you right now." She turned to Thomas. "We're taking one of the guest rooms. We won't be long."

"Don't worry about me," Thomas said. "I trust you. If you say Seamus is in good hands, then he's in good hands. Besides, you're in the same house. That's good enough for me."

Estelle led the way. Kaspar walked behind her, with Julian at his elbow. Julian hadn't said anything, but Kaspar knew he wanted to. He leaned closer, and when Julian looked at him, he shrugged. He didn't want to tell Julian he might be pregnant. He didn't want Julian to hope if it was only a stomach bug or something.

Estelle snatched a bag from one of the chairs in the entrance as they walked past it, then headed upstairs. Kaspar could hear the murmur of voices in a bedroom further down the hallway, and his stomach twisted. They entered one of the guest bedrooms, and Estelle made Julian close the door.

"So? What's going on?"

Kaspar looked at Julian. "I haven't been feeling well, and Julian and I have been trying for a baby."

Estelle's eyes brightened. "Really? That's good to hear." She opened her bag and rustled through it, then took out a pregnancy test. She held it out to Kaspar. "You know what to do."

Kaspar took the test with a trembling hand and headed to the bathroom. Julian stayed outside, and it was unnerving for Kaspar to have to do this on his own. Kaspar didn't want Julian to watch him pee on a stick, though, so this was better for everyone.

Of course, now that he *had* to pee, he didn't have to. Kaspar looked at the ceiling, rolling his eyes at himself. He turned on the water in the sink, then focused on what he had to do. Finally, he managed to pee on the stick.

But now that this was done, he had to wait again. He put the stick on the sink as he washed his hands, then stared at it. He didn't want to go outside without having an answer, and he was ready to wait for as long as it took. If he was about to be disappointed, he wanted to know before telling Julian.

But the answer was yes.

Kaspar's eyes smarted as two pink lines appeared on the test. It was positive. Kaspar was pregnant.

He snatched the test from the sink and opened the bathroom door. Julian and Estelle were there, and they both looked at him when he stepped out. Julian's posture was stiff, and he gave Kaspar a questioning glance. He looked like he might be about to faint, so Kaspar didn't make him wait. "It's positive," he said.

Julian's face broke into a smile that could have lit up the

sky. "Really? You're pregnant?"

Kaspar nodded. His throat felt tight, and he wasn't sure he could say anything else. He drew Julian into his arms and hugged him tight, unable to say anything.

They were about to become parents. They were having a baby.

"Congratulations, both of you," Estelle said. "Now, if you don't need anything else, I'll go back to Seamus. I forgot his water downstairs."

"Of course," Julian said. "Thank you."

"Actually," Kaspar interrupted. He looked away from Julian because he knew Julian would get angry. "Julian hasn't been feeling well lately."

Estelle frowned. "What do you mean?"

"He's been throwing up quite a bit."

"It's nothing," Julian protested. "Just stress and the new job. I'm perfectly fine."

Estelle arched a brow. "You don't *look* sick. Kaspar said you were trying for a baby, but have you *both* been trying to get pregnant?"

Julian blinked. "I can't get pregnant. You told me that."

Estelle's eyes widened. "What are you talking about?"

Julian bit his lower lip. "When you saw me after I first arrived at the Bishop House. You examined me, and you told me I couldn't get pregnant."

For the first time since he'd known her, Estelle looked shocked and worried. "That is *not* what I said, Julian," she said.

Julian frowned. "What are you talking about?"

"I never said you couldn't get pregnant. You can." She looked from Julian to Kaspar. "Actually, to me, it sounds like you might *be*."

Julian shook his head. "I don't understand. You said—I know I heard you say that I couldn't get pregnant."

Estelle's expression softened. "Oh, Julian. No. I never said you couldn't get pregnant again. I never said it because it's not the truth. You can get pregnant. Have you been using protection?"

"No. I thought—"

"You thought you couldn't get pregnant."

Julian had truly believed that, and he'd told Kaspar. Now, it sounded like it might not be true, and Kaspar wasn't sure what to make of the news.

Julian didn't understand what Estelle was saying. "I heard you. You said I couldn't get pregnant." He was repeating himself, but then, his thoughts were repeating themselves in his mind, round and round until he couldn't understand anything.

Estelle glared at him and put her hands on her hips. "I said that between your age and the fact that you had Kari on your own and that your first pregnancy and birth weren't medicalized, it would be *hard* for you to get pregnant. It was entirely possible, though." She eyed his stomach. "And I'm pretty sure you managed."

Julian's hand flew to his stomach. "Are you sure?"

Estelle's scowl deepened. "Are you telling me I don't remember what I said?"

"Of course not. I just—I thought—I was so sure you said I couldn't have children."

Estelle's scowl softened. "I'm really sorry. It's obvious I should have been clearer, and that I should have talked to you again after that first visit. Is this a bad thing? The fact that you're pregnant, I mean. You were happy about Kaspar, but a second baby might be too much, especially if you thought you couldn't get pregnant."

Was it a bad thing? Julian had no idea. He'd been so

convinced that he would never get pregnant again that he had never thought about having another baby, or rather, about carrying another baby. He and Kaspar hadn't talked about it, since they both thought it was impossible. Julian had no idea how Kaspar would react, especially since he was pregnant.

Looking at Kaspar right now was one of the scariest things Julian could remember doing. The way Kaspar would react to this would make or break Julian's life. He could have this baby on his own if he was pregnant. He knew that. He'd done it with Kari, and he would do it again if he had to.

But he didn't want to. He loved Kaspar, and they'd been planning a life together. He didn't want to lose that. He didn't want to lose a future he'd finally allowed himself to dream of.

Julian looked at Kaspar. It was hard for him to read Kaspar's expression in the beginning, but then Kaspar smiled, and Julian knew everything would be okay.

Or at least, he hoped so.

"Why don't you go in the bathroom and take a pregnancy test?" Estelle asked. "I don't need to visit either of you today, so I'm going to go back downstairs to Seamus. Let me know if it's positive. If it is, we can plan something together so I can visit both of you sometime in the next few weeks."

Julian frowned. "And if it's negative?"

Estelle grimaced. "Then, I want to see you as soon as possible. Kaspar said you've been throwing up?"

"Yes. I've also had some backaches, and I'm exhausted, but I didn't think it was pregnancy. I thought I was stressed and overworked."

"It's a possibility, but if the test comes back negative, I want to see you tomorrow or the day after that."

Julian couldn't even think about that possibility. He didn't want to, not until he took the test. He nodded at Estelle and accepted the test she handed him, then watched her leave. He turned to Kaspar, who gestured to the bathroom. "I'll be right here," he said.

"Are you sure? Because I know you didn't sign up for this. We were planning to have one baby, not two."

Kaspar nodded. "I'm sure. Whether you're pregnant or have a health problem, I'm not going anywhere. I promise."

Kaspar's words helped settle something in Julian's mind. He took a deep breath and stepped into the bathroom, closing the door behind himself. He put his hands onto the sink and looked down at the pregnancy test. He swallowed, but it didn't make things easier. He was confused and worried and feeling a mixture of emotions that he didn't know how to deal with right now. He might be pregnant. At forty-two, after living for more than twenty-six years in the forest on his own, after having one child who was now pregnant with Julian's grandchild, he might be having a baby.

Julian had no idea what to do with that information. It was another thing he hadn't allowed himself to think about. In the beginning, it had been because, well, he'd been alone. He'd been living in the forest, and he knew how hard it was to be pregnant and have a baby on his own. Besides, how would he have gotten pregnant? Then, once he'd arrived at the Bishop House, he'd thought that Estelle had told him that he couldn't have children. He'd made his peace with it.

And now, everything was upside down.

He picked up the pregnancy test with a still-trembling hand and opened the box. He'd never done this before. When he'd been pregnant with Kari, he'd realized he was pregnant because of how his body had behaved. He'd been throwing up then, too, and now that he thought about it, he'd had the same backache. He'd been terrified. He'd known that if the alpha found out that he was carrying his child, he would have locked him up until he gave birth. Julian had refused to raise his child in that kind of situation. Hell, he was pretty sure that he wouldn't have been able to raise Kari at all if he'd stayed home. The alpha would've taken Kari as soon as Julian had given birth, and he would have raised him with his wife.

That was why Julian had left. His life had been hard, but he was still convinced that he'd done the right thing. Having this baby would be so entirely different. It would be a new experience for him, especially with Kaspar also pregnant.

Even though Julian had never used a pregnancy test, he knew how they worked. He peed on the stick and put it on the sink, trying to avoid looking at it while he washed his hands. It was hard not to, but he knew staring wouldn't give him an answer faster.

Then two lines appeared, and Julian almost fell to his knees. He was pregnant. He was carrying Kaspar's baby.

He pressed both hands to his stomach, and his eyes filled with tears. He knew he needed to leave the bathroom and tell Kaspar about this, but he didn't think he would be able to get a word out. He wasn't sure he could talk around the emotion that clung to his throat, closing it and making it feel tight.

He sat on the floor because his legs wouldn't hold him up for much longer. They felt like rubber and trembled with emotion. He leaned against the wall, welcoming the coolness of the tile, and closed his eyes.

A knock on the door interrupted his thoughts. "Julian? Is everything okay?"

Julian hadn't locked the door, so he called out, "Yes. Come in. Please."

The door opened, and Kaspar's eyes widened when he saw Julian on the floor. He knelt next to him, wrapping his arms around him. "What is it? What happened?"

Julian didn't want him to panic, especially since he was pregnant. "I'm fine."

"The test?"

"It's positive. I'm pregnant." Julian leaned back and rubbed his face. He looked at Kaspar, even though he was terrified. "I know you never signed up for two babies. If you want — "

Kaspar shook his head, cupped Julian's cheeks with both hands, and kissed him. For a few seconds, Julian was able to forget about everything that wasn't Kaspar. Reality came back soon, though, and he gently pushed Kaspar away. "Like I was saying, I know you didn't sign up for two babies."

"I signed up to be with you," Kaspar told him. "I don't care what that implies. I'm not going anywhere. I'm having your baby, and you're having mine. We might not have planned for two babies, but we can deal with it. We would if it were twins, right?"

Julian's eyes widened. "God. What if one of us is carrying twins?"

To his surprise, instead of being struck in horror, Kaspar laughed. "Then we'll deal with it. I don't care how many babies we have. I love you, Julian. I want to build this family with you. I'm not going anywhere. I promise. It might not be what we expected, but we can make it work. We have friends and a family. You have a new job. It won't be easy, but it doesn't mean we won't be happy." He hesitated. "Because you are, right? I know you thought you couldn't have children, but now you're pregnant. How do you feel about that?"

Julian hadn't thought about it yet. How did he feel about carrying another baby? About giving birth a second time? "I'm happy." Happier than he'd ever thought he would be. He had a job, freedom, a family, and love. It would be hard, but he was used to hard, especially when he knew it would be *so* worth it.

CHAPTER TWELVE

Julian was still in shock by the time the evening came, but it was easy to get distracted when the first cries of baby Scarlet echoed through the house.

He and Kaspar were in the living room, and they stayed right where they were. Julian remembered too well how he'd felt when Kari was born. This situation was nothing like the one he'd been in, but he knew Seamus and Alex would want some time alone with Scarlet. They probably wouldn't want to see anyone until tomorrow, so he was wondering if he and Kaspar should go home when Alex appeared at the living room door.

He looked tired but also happy. He was *beaming*. When Kaspar rose from the couch, Alex grabbed him and wrapped his arms around him, shocking both Kaspar and Julian.

They both knew Alex, of course, but Julian wouldn't have said they were friends with him. He was a good man, though, and Julian was more than happy to hug him and congratulate him when he released Kaspar and turned toward him. "Are they both okay?" he asked.

Alex nodded as he stepped away. "They're both perfect. She's so beautiful. She has all this black hair, and I *swear* she was smiling."

Julian doubted that, but he didn't say anything. Alex was a new father, and everything his daughter did would make him marvel.

"We're happy for both of you. Tell Seamus that, will you?"

Alex frowned. "Why don't you tell him yourself?"

"I thought we should go home. I'm sure you and Seamus want some time alone with your daughter."

Alex blinked. "God, that sounds so weird. My *daughter*. I have a daughter."

Julian laughed. "It's going to take a while to get used to it. It's a huge change."

"It is. I mean, I knew it would be, but now that she's here, it's different." Alex rubbed his face. He looked exhausted, but happiness shone from him. "Come on. Seamus wants to see you."

Julian was surprised. "Are you sure?"

"I think he wants to thank you. You were there for him when he was terrified."

Julian was humbled by the trust Seamus was showing in him. He knew Seamus and Alex would want to protect Scarlet and to keep people away from her, especially in the first few days. When he'd had Kari, he'd been lucky, since he hadn't had anyone to barge into his little two-person family life, but they wouldn't be as lucky. Alex was the future alpha. As soon as the news that he'd had a child spread, everyone would come to congratulate him and take a peek at baby Scarlet. These were the last few hours of peace Alex and Seamus had, yet they were inviting Julian and Kaspar to be part of them.

Julian didn't protest. If Seamus wanted to see him, then he would. He and Kaspar followed Alex back to the bedroom in which Seamus had given birth. It was the bedroom he and Alex shared, and Julian felt slightly awkward stepping in, even though there were plenty of people there.

The bedroom was still busy. Estelle and Patrick were putting away things and cleaning, while Hope, Alex's mother, was cooing over the baby. Seamus was holding Scarlet, and he looked tired but happy and at peace. He couldn't seem to stop smiling, and it made Julian smile, too.

Seamus looked up when he heard them walk in, and his

smile widened. "Julian. I was worried you'd already left. I'm surprised you waited so long. It's late."

Julian shrugged. If he was honest with himself, he hadn't stayed because he wanted to be there when Scarlet was born. He and Kaspar had stuck around because they were still in shock over their own news. He'd wanted some time alone with Kaspar, and the Bishop House was the last place in which they could have that. It was always busy with people, so it had been good for them to have a few hours on their own, even if it had been in a house that wasn't theirs.

"I'm going to get a snack for you," Hope said. She was giving them some time, and Julian was grateful.

With everything that was going on, he felt especially vulnerable and emotional at the thought of meeting Scarlet for the first time. He didn't want to start crying in front of Hope.

Estelle looked at Julian once Hope was gone. "So?"

Julian bit his lower lip. He hadn't been planning to announce that he and Kaspar were having two babies just yet, but for whatever reason, he found it impossible to keep the secret. Besides, it wasn't exactly a secret. He would start to show soon. He'd ignored the symptoms, but he was pretty sure he'd gotten pregnant one of the first times he and Kaspar had made love. "It was positive."

Estelle beamed. "I'm happy for both of you. Call me tomorrow or the day after that. We'll set up a visit. I need to keep an eye on you, especially considering your background."

Julian laughed. "You mean my age."

Estelle shrugged. "That, and the fact that you had Kari on your own in the forest. You're lucky things went the way they did."

"What's she talking about?" Seamus asked when Julian turned his attention back to him. Julian and Kaspar exchanged a glance. Julian didn't want to blurt out the news if Kaspar wasn't okay with it, but Kaspar nodded, and Julian knew what it meant.

He pressed a hand to his stomach. It still looked the same, but it wouldn't for long. "I'm pregnant."

Seamus' eyes widened. "Oh my God. I would hug you if I could get out of this bed. I'm sorry, but I'm not feeling up to that. But I'm so happy for you!"

Julian laughed. "Don't worry about it and stay right where you are. I remember all too well what it was like to give birth."

"This is great news."

Kaspar cleared his throat. "I'm pregnant, too."

Seamus blinked and cocked his head. "You decided to have two babies at the same time?" He snapped his mouth shut. "Sorry. I didn't mean to be rude."

"You weren't rude," Kaspar said with a smile. "It was a surprise. We were trying to have a baby, but we didn't think Julian could have any more kids. His pregnancy *is* a surprise, but we're happy."

"Of course you're happy," Alex said. "Babies always make people happy. You can't stay at the Bishop House, though."

Julian hadn't expected the conversation to go that way. "We're fine there."

"For now, sure. But now that you can leave, you should probably have your own home, especially with two babies on the way. Who's further along?"

"I am," Julian said.

Alex nodded. "I see. I need to talk to my father about assigning you another bodyguard."

"I'm sorry?" Julian had no idea what was happening.

"People in the council have accepted you so far because you weren't pregnant and it was easy for them to ignore the fact that you're a carrier, but I want to be sure that none of them are going to change their mind or try anything when they find out you're pregnant, especially with what Jacqueline just tried to pull. But enough talking about that right now.

Where do you want to live? How about a house close by? That way, you can have as much help as you want when the babies arrive. Besides, they won't be much younger than Scarlet. We can have playdates when they're older."

Alex was rushing ahead, but Julian understood where that need came from. He'd started a new chapter of his life, and he was eager to see what would happen.

Julian felt the same way.

"I think it's a good idea," Julian said slowly. "I love the Bishop House, but maybe it *is* time for us to have our own house, since we're starting a family." He looked at Kaspar, but he already knew Kaspar would agree. It made sense, even though Julian was sad at the thought of leaving the Bishop House and the carriers who still lived there behind.

"I don't know if there's a house available. I'll have to ask my dad," Alex said. "But if there isn't, we'll build it. I want our kids to grow up together. They're the next generation. Scarlet will be the next alpha, and you two are both carriers having babies together. We're leaving prejudice and bigotry behind, and those kids are the symbol of that."

He wasn't wrong. Having these babies was the beginning of something new, something big for the entire forest. Julian wasn't sure he liked his babies being a symbol, but there was nothing he could do about it. He would shield them and protect them, but beyond that, he didn't know what would happen.

CHAPTER THIRTEEN

When Julian opened his eyes the next morning, he was already smiling. He doubted he would stop smiling for a long time. Whatever happened, whatever people told him, he was happy. He had Kaspar, and they would have two babies soon. What more could he want from life?

"You look like I feel," Kaspar murmured against the skin of Julian's neck.

Julian turned around in Kaspar's arms so they could face each other. "You mean happy?"

Kaspar nodded. "It still weird, but yeah. I'm happy. I guess the worry will start soon, so I'm going to enjoy this as much as I can in the meantime."

"I know worrying is inevitable. But compared to when I had Kari, this is going to be a walk in the park."

Kaspar laughed. "For you, maybe. But this is my first baby, and by the time she or he is born, we'll already have yours. We'll have a newborn, and I'll go into labor, and oh my God, how are we going to deal with that?"

Kaspar was starting to panic, which was the last thing Julian wanted. He cupped Kaspar's cheeks with both his hands and waited until Kaspar finally managed to breathe in and out more calmly. "We won't be alone," he said. "You heard Alex. He wants us to move closer to him and Seamus. Besides, we'll have the entire cete by our side. You know what that means. We'll have dozens of babysitters if we need one. And I will be right there with you when you give birth. I promise."

"What if we give birth at the same time? I mean, Seamus

had Scarlet a month early. What if that happens to me?"

"Then we'll deal with it. We'll hold hands while we push. I know this is terrifying, but you have to remember that we're not alone."

Their bedroom door slammed open, startling both of them. Julian scrambled into a sitting position, pulling the sheet around his body, his eyes wide. He only relaxed when he saw that Kari was walking in, looking around as if he expected someone to attack him.

"I know I raised you in a forest, but I taught you to knock on doors, didn't I?" Julian said.

Kari made a beeline for him. He ignored Kaspar and climbed onto the bed on Julian's empty side, snuggling against him. "What's going on? You were sick yesterday. What happened? Are you still feeling sick? What did Estelle say? You talked to her, right?"

Too many questions—Julian blinked. He should have known someone would tattle to Kari that he hadn't been feeling well. He was surprised it had taken so long. "I'm okay."

"Are you sure? Because I can get Estelle right now if you need her."

Sometimes, Julian wondered if his relationship with Kari was normal. They were very close, and Kari hadn't thought twice about climbing onto the bed, even though Kaspar was there. He was an adult, yet he was wrapped around Julian. Julian knew that wasn't normal, but he also knew it was because of the way Kari had been raised. Julian hadn't had a choice. He'd been the only person in his son's life for so long, and it still had a big impact on Kari and how he behaved.

"He's fine," Kaspar said. He didn't look annoyed or angry at Kari's presence. Julian was relieved. He and Kari were slowly growing apart, but it would take a while for Kari to stop feeling like Julian was the only person in his life. He had Calder, of course, but he still tended to come straight to Julian when he needed him.

"Are you sure?" Kari sat up and looked both at Julian and Kaspar. "I'm sorry. I know I shouldn't have barged in. Calder told me to slow down, but I was worried."

"You don't have to apologize. I know you love your dad and that you worry about him," Kaspar said. He grinned. "The next time, you really should knock. That way, we can put on underwear before you come in."

Kari grimaced. "I didn't need to know that. Now I'm going to have nightmares. I should go and leave you to whatever you were doing before I got here."

"He's kidding," Julian reassured him. "We're wearing pajama pants. Don't worry." He hesitated. He wasn't sure how Kari would take their news. He had seemed to be okay with it when they talked about the possibility, but now that things were becoming a reality, he couldn't help but wonder. Still, he had to tell Kari about this before Kari found out from someone else. "I'd like you to stay. We have to tell you something."

Kari sat cross-legged and looked at them. "Did you do it? Did you get Kaspar pregnant?" He grimaced again. "Actually, I'm not sure I want to know. I don't want to imagine how you got him pregnant."

Julian reached out and gently slapped the back of Kari's head. "Then don't. How do you think I feel when I think about you getting pregnant? But yes. Kaspar *is* pregnant." Julian paused and sucked in a breath. "And so am I."

Kari blinked. "I thought you couldn't get pregnant again."

"I thought so too, but apparently, I misheard. Estelle said that she told me it would be *hard* for me to get pregnant considering everything, but not that it was impossible."

Kari grinned. "So your baby was an accident?"

Julian slapped him again. "Never call your brother or sister an accident."

Kari paled and pressed his hands against his stomach.

"Holy shit. I'm going to have two siblings, and they're only going to be a few months younger than my own baby. We're a fucked-up family." He grinned. "But we're a family. Can you believe that, Dad? We have a family."

Some days, Julian had a hard time wrapping his mind around that. "We have a family," he confirmed.

"We're going to raise them together, right? I mean, I'm pretty sure you and Kaspar are going to need help, especially with your job."

"We haven't talked about this yet," Kaspar said. He wrapped an arm around Julian's shoulders and pulled him close, kissing his temple. "We only found out we were pregnant yesterday. But Alex already suggested we move closer to the alpha's house, and we agreed. We want to be close by, especially since Scarlet will be about the same age as our kids. The three of them and yours can grow up together."

"I never thought this would happen," Kari said wistfully. "Some days, I'm still not convinced it's real."

It hurt Julian's heart a little. He'd done his best with Kari. He'd raised him as well as he could have, but he knew he was only one man. Kari had missed a lot of things while growing up, and hopefully, his life now made up for it. "I know. It's hard to believe, but we *do* have all of this now."

"I can't believe that my dad is pregnant at forty-two. Jesus. Our family is going to be a weird one." He grinned fiercely. "But I'm the only one who can say that. Anyone else, I'm kicking their asses."

Julian laughed. He wasn't offended by the age thing. He knew he was old to have a child, especially with how Kari's birth had gone. But it had been decades since he'd had Kari, and he felt ready for this new baby. He knew it would probably be his last, but that was okay. If he and Kaspar wanted more children, Kaspar could carry them. Giving birth wasn't as important as Julian had believed. Whoever did it, it didn't take anything away from the other father. He'd never thought about it that way because he'd only ever been a single dad, but he could see how true that was now.

"So, have you already picked the names?" Kari asked. "Personally, I think you should stick with the K thing. I mean, you have Kaspar and me. How about Karina? Kayla? Kermit? No, I don't like that one. Kenneth?"

Julian laughed and shook his head. He shouldn't have worried about how Kari would take the news. His son was happy for him, and that made *him* happier than he'd ever been. "We haven't thought about it yet. Besides, we have time."

"Then you can start. Calder and I have been talking about names, too, but all the names he wants suck, and by that, I mean that they aren't the names *I* want."

Julian leaned back against his pillows and listened to Kari babble about Calder's suggestions. This was his life now, and he couldn't have been happier.

Kaspar, Julian, and Kari headed downstairs after about an hour. Kari had allowed Kaspar and Julian to wash up and dress — thank God — and they'd waited until the breakfast crowd had dissipated. Kaspar felt slightly guilty at not being on the move yet, taking care of cleaning the house or planning meals, but he felt that both he and Julian deserved to take a day off after the night they'd had. Besides, there were more than enough people in the house. Someone else could cook or empty the dishwasher.

"Why don't the two of you head to the living room?" he told Julian and Kari. "I'll go to the kitchen to grab something to eat."

"I'll come help you," Julian suggested.

Kaspar shook his head. "Don't worry. Go sit with your son. I'm sure you won't mind some alone time with him."

Kari hooked his arm around Julian's and pulled him away. "You're right. We don't mind. Thank you."

Kaspar watched them walk away, slightly bemused. That was how he generally seemed to feel when Kari was involved. He knew Kari would always be a part of his life, but even though Kari could be a sweetheart and obviously loved his dad, he was also fucking weird.

Kaspar went to the kitchen and got started on breakfast. Since they would eat in the living room and it was late, he didn't want to go overboard, so he limited himself to making a few peanut butter and jelly sandwiches and grabbing orange juice from the fridge. When he got to the living room with his tray, Julian and Kari were sitting next to each other with their heads close as they talked.

Kaspar paused for a moment to watch them. He'd never realized how much they looked like each other, and it was a bit weird. Julian was like an older version of Kari, with a few more wrinkles and some gray hair, but to Kaspar, he was the most gorgeous of the two. No matter how similar they looked, Kaspar could never have fallen in love with Kari. He was harder than Julian, strong-willed and provocative. He knew what he wanted, and he never hesitated to say out loud exactly what he thought, and in detail. Julian, on the other hand, was gentler and softer, and it amazed Kaspar that he was like that after everything he'd gone through.

It was true that the rape had happened twenty-six years before, but still. It was an experience that would have changed anyone, and it had no doubt changed Julian. It was hard to see how, though. Kaspar hadn't known Julian back then. He hadn't even been born. Julian had been a teenager, and he'd spent the following twenty-six years alone. Who knew who he would have become if those things hadn't happened?

But he wouldn't have been Kaspar's then. He wouldn't

have been who he was now, the man Kaspar was in love with. It was a moot point. Julian would never get back what he'd lost, but that didn't mean he couldn't have a future.

Kaspar saw something move from the corner of his eye, but when he turned, no one was there. He huffed at himself and finally walked into the living room. Julian looked up and smiled at him, and like always, it made Kaspar's heart go pitter-patter.

Julian started to rise to his feet, but Kaspar shook his head. "Stay there." He put the tray onto the coffee table. "I didn't know what you wanted, Kari, but I can go back to the kitchen."

Kari snatched one of the sandwiches from the tray and settled back against the couch, rubbing his stomach. "This is perfect. Thank you."

Kaspar settled down. It was always strange to be with Julian and Kari together. They were a unit, and they tended to isolate themselves. Kaspar doubted they even realized they did. They were so used to being each other's entire life that it was instinctive to them. Kaspar didn't mind. Julian had told him a lot of things about his and Kari's life in the forest, and Kaspar had been horrified at most of it. He fully understood why Julian and Kari were so close.

"So, what's next for you?" Kari asked around a mouthful of bread, peanut butter, and jelly.

Julian glared at him. "I'm pretty sure I taught you to eat with your mouth closed, too."

Kari shrugged and grinned, showing Julian his stained teeth. Julian rolled his eyes and focused on his breakfast.

"We should probably talk to Thomas," Kaspar said. "I know Alex offered to find us a house, but Thomas is still the alpha. I doubt he'll object to us moving out of here, but he needs to know. Besides, he's probably the best person to ask where we can find an empty house."

"Alex said we might have to have one built," Julian said. "There won't be a lot of time, though. Nine months seem long, but we don't even have that."

Kari bounced on the couch. "I think there's an empty house close to Calder's." He paused and looked at Kaspar. "Unless you don't want to live that close to me?"

Kaspar blinked. "Why wouldn't I?"

Kari shrugged. "I don't know. Some people think that Dad and I should put more distance between us. That I'm an adult and that I shouldn't be so close to him."

Kaspar wasn't surprised. He *was* surprised that someone had mentioned that to Kari, and he couldn't help but wonder if whoever had done so was still breathing. He knew he needed to be very careful about what he was about to say. He had to keep a balance between what he wanted, and what would be right for Julian and Kari. "I don't mind living next door to you. I think it would make Julian happy, and when he's happy, I am, too. Besides, our children might be your kid's uncles or aunts, but we'll raise them like cousins, and I want them to be that close. I could do without you barging into our bedroom, though."

Kari nibbled on his lower lip. "So the only thing you have against my relationship with my dad is that I don't knock?"

"I love that you and your father are close, and I don't care what other people say. I don't expect the two of you to put distance between you or something like that. I *do* expect you to knock on private doors, though. I don't care if you walk into our kitchen or whatever without waiting for us to invite you in, but bedrooms are different." Kaspar grinned. "Although if I have it my way, you might walk in on something you don't want to see even in the kitchen."

Kari paled. "I'll knock. I promise."

Kaspar nodded. "Then we're okay."

The relief on Kari's face was obvious, and surprising, since

Kari didn't like to show how he felt to anyone but his dad and Calder. Kaspar was humbled to see that Kari trusted him, too.

Kari stuffed the last bite of his sandwich into his mouth. "Good. So when are you talking to Thomas? And Estelle? You both need to see her. Especially you, Dad."

"Will you stop implying I'm old?" Julian grumbled, but there was no heat in the words.

"I never said anything about you being old!"

Kaspar leaned back against the couch and munched on his sandwich as he listened to them. He would never get rid of Kari, not if he wanted Julian in his life, so he supposed he should get used to this kind of conversation.

Julian watched Kari climb down the porch steps. His pregnancy was getting more obvious, and it made Julian happy. It also reminded him that he was pregnant, too, that he would soon be in Kari's position. God, there was so much to do. He and Kaspar needed to find a home, to get furniture, to get ready for two babies. He wasn't sure how they would manage to do that with so little time left, especially with his job, but they would have to.

And that was without even considering what would happen once the babies were born. Julian would have to take time off, of course, but he hated to think about Kaspar alone at home with two newborns once he inevitably went back to work.

Julian waved one last time, then he stepped back into the house and closed the door. He turned to go back to the living room, where he, Kari, and Kaspar had talked for the better part of the morning. They'd had a nice chat, and it was one of the things that Julian missed the most about being with his son. He and Kari were used to spending so much time together that it was still weird not to see him every day. He was close by, though, so they could if they wanted to, but they were both busy.

To Julian's surprise, Calum was in the living room when he stepped in. Kaspar was still on the couch, dozing, and Julian went to sit next to him. He eyed Calum, wondering what was happening. He wasn't about to ask, even though Calum was kind of creeping him out, hovering by the door and watching them.

After a few moments, he couldn't stop himself. "Do you need anything?" he asked.

Kaspar jerked, then sat up, rubbing his eyes. "What?" he asked.

Julian patted his knee. "Not you. Calum."

Kaspar blinked. "Calum is here?"

"I wasn't spying, I swear," Calum said.

"I never said you were spying."

Calum bit his lower lip and stepped closer. "I wasn't spying, but I heard you talking with your son."

"Yes?" Julian could only imagine what Calum had heard. It wasn't like he remembered every single thing he'd told Kari.

"You told him you and Kaspar were going to leave the Bishop House."

Julian hadn't expected that, but then he hadn't expected Calum to talk to him. The bat shifter always kept to himself. He had one of the single rooms, and Julian didn't think he'd seen him more than a handful of times since he'd arrived at the Bishop House. Calum stayed in his bedroom as much as he could, coming down only for meals, and even then, he'd snatched the food and gone back upstairs more than once.

"Is it true? Are you leaving?" Calum asked.

Julian looked at Kaspar, who shrugged. Kaspar had been at the Bishop House longer than Julian, so he knew Calum better, but Julian doubted *anyone* knew Calum well.

"Well, Julian and I are both pregnant," Kaspar said. "We'll have two babies very close together, and we'll need help, as well as a more private space for our family."

Calum nodded. "Of course. There are too many people here." He sucked in a breath. "I want to go with you. I want to live with you."

Julian's mouth fell open. *This*, he really hadn't expected. "You want to live with us?"

Calum stepped closer. "I promise I won't bug you. I'll take care of the babies. I'll be a live-in babysitter. Just, please, say yes. I can't go home."

Julian raised his hand and gestured toward the second couch. "Why don't you sit down and talk to us? I'm not saying no, but I'd like to understand what's going on and why you suddenly want to come with Kaspar and me when you've barely talked to me since I arrived." And Julian didn't think Calum had talked to Kaspar any more than he had to him.

Calum sat on the edge of the couch as if he expected to have to bolt at any second. "You know what happened when the cete was attacked."

"I was here. I know."

"So you know that the bats abandoned the cete. They stood back when they were needed, even though the cete helped them by taking me in. My alpha thinks that being on the right side of the council is the only thing he needs to do, but I don't think that's true. It's a good thing, of course, but he should have done more, considering what the cete is doing for him." He swallowed. "The cete gave me a home when no one else would. I know I haven't been grateful or anything like that. I stayed by myself because I was afraid. And I still am. I'm terrified of losing all of this. Some days I still can't believe I have it. But what the bats did wasn't fair. They should have helped the cete. I don't want to go back, and now that there are new laws in place, I don't have to. But I also don't have any other place to go."

"Thomas won't ask you to leave the Bishop House anytime soon if you don't want to," Kaspar pointed out. "You know he's not that kind of person."

"I know. But I hate feeling useless. I hate feeling the way I feel now, as if no one likes me. And I know it's because of the way I behave. I understand that, and I'll try to change. But I don't like living here. There are too many people, too much noise."

Julian couldn't help but smile. "You do know how much noise two babies make, right?"

"I know, but it's different. And I promise I *can* help you with the babies. I'll take care of them, and I'll do the housework and everything else."

"You don't have to make those kinds of promises."

"I know. I just want to go with you."

Julian looked at Kaspar. He wasn't sure he could make that kind of promise, but he wanted to. He'd just been thinking that he and Kaspar would need help once the babies arrive, and probably toward the end of their pregnancies, too. It would be easier for them to have someone who lived in the house with them, that was for sure.

But would Calum be the right choice? Julian didn't know. He didn't know enough about Calum to be sure. Now was the time to get to know him, though. Julian and Kaspar still lived in the Bishop House, and they would for a little while.

"How about this," he started. "You just said yourself that you're a loner, and I don't expect you to change. I understand how overwhelming the Bishop House can be. But I'd like to get to know you before I make any kind of promise. You might not be a good fit for us, or the babies. Also, I don't want to be rude, but I don't think I could leave my babies with someone I don't trust."

Calum nodded. "I understand. And I know that saying you

can trust me won't make it happen. But you can get to know me if you want. There's time. You're not even showing yet."

"That's what I was thinking. We can talk, see if we work well together, and once Kaspar and I find another house, we'll revisit this conversation and decide what's next. But two babies are a lot of work."

"That's why you need me. There will be three of us. I could take care of night feedings or whatever. I'll do just about anything. I'll help."

He wasn't wrong. Julian looked at Kaspar again. He was pretty sure that Kaspar thought the same, but he wanted to be sure. He didn't want to make any promises he wouldn't be able to keep.

Kaspar nodded. "That's fine with me. I've been here longer than you, Julian, and I do like Calum, even though he's a bit of a bitchy guy."

Calum blushed fiercely. "I'm sorry if I was ever rude to you."

"Don't worry about that. But it's obvious we don't know each other as well as we should, and I look forward to changing that."

"So do I."

"Good. Then we'll be okay." Kaspar smiled. "Welcome to the family, Calum."

Julian had no idea where this would go, but he felt good about it. If he and Kaspar could give Calum the help he obviously needed while getting the help they needed, too, it had to be a good thing, right?

CHAPTER FOURTEEN

Julian really could have done without this meeting. His back ached, and it meant he hadn't been able to sleep well last night. He was tired and sleepy, and he couldn't wait to get home and back into bed with Kaspar. But instead he had to be here — at a meeting with the human team — to find out what Luther had discovered about Randy and Jacqueline. Julian was curious, but not so curious that he wouldn't rather be at home.

Calder gently elbowed him in the side. "At least try to look like you're interested," he murmured

"I *am* interested." He wasn't. The bat council member was talking about something or other, and Julian was bored to death. He was here to see Luther, but that was all, at least for today. "I'm also tired, though," Julian told him.

Calder grinned. "Kaspar kept you up last night?"

Julian rolled his eyes. "You're my son-in-law. I'm not talking about that kind of stuff with you. And no. The baby keeps me up at night."

Calder's gaze slid down to Julian's stomach. "Already?"

Julian shrugged. "Not the baby himself, but backache and stuff like that."

"Are you okay?"

"I will be." But Julian was touched by Calder's worry. They really were a family, weren't they? He was a good man for Kari, and Julian was glad his son had chosen well.

"Kari is always complaining about something. I never realized that pregnancy could be so hard."

Julian chuckled. "Kari is a complainer. He complains about everything, even if it's fine. He likes the attention, especially coming from you."

"I don't mind. I want to take care of him, but he's a hard man to take care of."

Julian wasn't surprised, but he liked that Calder wasn't giving up. Kari needed more people to take care of him. Calder was the perfect man to do that.

A knock on the door made Julian sigh in relief. Maybe they would be able to go to lunch, after all. If he couldn't go back to bed, he at least wanted food, and Kaspar was waiting for him.

The door opened, and Luther walked in, a few of his team members right behind him. The others stayed outside, and Julian prayed that Kari wouldn't try to bash their skulls together or something like that. Julian wouldn't be surprised. He wasn't sure it was a good idea to have Kaspar and Kari wait for him and Calder out there, but they were having lunch together once this was over, and this was the easiest way to make that happen. They wouldn't have to go back to cete territory to pick Kaspar and Kari up, but it also put Kari in the path of a lot of people he might want to kill.

"Thank you for meeting with me," Luther said. He sat down in the chair in front of Calder and nodded at the council members around the table. Not all of them were there, but Calder was because Luther wanted to talk about what happened in cete territory.

Calder leaned over the table. "Can you tell me what happened?"

Luther looked uncomfortable, which was new. Julian didn't know him well, of course, but he'd never seen the man be anything other than sure of himself. "Again, I apologize. I should have thought about what I was doing before doing it. But I acted on what one of my team members told me, and I trusted him."

Calder leaned back in his chair. "Of course you did. He was part of your team. I don't blame you for trusting him, or for coming to cete territory. Nothing irreparable was done, even though you were rude. I would just like to know what happened."

"Of course. In the beginning, Randy stuck to his story that someone he didn't know had called him and told him that the cete and the sleuth were planning something. It didn't take him long to tell the truth, though. Apparently, that someone's name is Jacqueline. It wasn't the first time they spoke."

"She was the coyote council member."

"I remember her," Luther confirmed.

"We expected her to create problems, especially after she lost her role as the coyote council member. We didn't think she would try to use your team to do it, though."

Luther nodded curtly. "Apparently, she talked to Randy one of the first times we were here. She cornered him when he was alone, and she talked him into doing this. I never realized that Randy had something against shifters. I apologize for what he said. He was a new team member, and while I trusted him, I should have known better. Jacqueline had an easy task with him because of how he feels about shifters, and that shouldn't have happened."

Calder waved his words away. "Don't worry about that. What did Jacqueline want to obtain by doing what she did?"

The corner of Luther's lips curled into a half-smile. "You should be the one answering that. You know her better than I do. I only know that she tried to use one of my team members, and I'm not happy about that."

"Well, she's used to being in power. You probably don't know a lot about how things were in the forest until very recently."

"You're right. I don't."

"Just like I suspect happens with humans, part of the council was in this for power and money, while the other part was trying to make sure the people in the forest had the best life possible. Until recently, the former had the majority on the council. There was nothing we could do. We had to work around them, and it wasn't easy. Jacqueline was one of those. She was exclusively on the council for power and to make sure that the coyote alpha had everything he wanted. She allowed him to torture and abuse his son. She and the council members on their side allowed a lot of people to be abused. Then the balance tipped. They lost a few council members, and we got the majority back. We created new laws, and she had to accept them, just like we accepted the way she and the others were doing things before because we couldn't do anything about it. She's angry. She wants her power back, and apparently, she's ready to do just about anything to make that happen."

Luther tapped his fingertips on the table. "But she's not a council member anymore."

"She's not. I know better than to hope that will be the end of it, but it will hinder her, at least in the beginning. But as you saw, she's already thinking about revenge, and she won't stop trying just because we found out. What happened to Randy?"

"I sent him home. I can't have him here if I don't trust him. I told him he was lucky because he didn't get killed on the spot when he said those things."

"We wouldn't touch a human. You don't follow the same laws we do."

Luther hesitated, then seemed to think better about whatever he was about to ask and didn't. "The rest of my team and I aren't going anywhere, though. We're staying for a while, and I want to be able to live with you. I realize we are guests, even though you're obligated to welcome us. Unfortunately, there's nothing either of us can do about that. I could tell my boss I don't want this job anymore, but he would send someone else."

Julian grimaced. There was no way for them to know who that someone else would be or how they would behave. If they were lucky, they would be a good person like Luther was. If they weren't, they might be more like Randy, and that was the last thing they needed.

He cleared his throat. "You need to keep an eye on us."

Luther's attention turned to him. "We do. Unfortunately, it's our job. But I hope we can learn from each other. Just like you had never met a human being before we arrived, we had never met a shifter. I think it could be a great learning opportunity for the entire team, and I'm looking forward to it."

Julian wasn't too sure about that. Luther might want to learn about shifters and their customs, but he doubted that most of his team would get behind that. Still, as long as they weren't like Randy and didn't try to sabotage this, he didn't care much. It wasn't like they had a choice anyway. Luther seemed to be a good person, and if this was what he wanted, then it was what he would get. It was better than the alternative.

It was better than losing the forest to humans who hated them.

Kaspar was relieved when the door to the council room opened and people started to walk out. He and Kari were waiting for Julian and Calder, and the rest of the human team was staring at them.

Or rather, they were staring at Kari, and Kaspar was pretty sure that smoke was going to start coming out of Kari's ears eventually if they didn't stop.

"I swear, it's almost like they've never seen a pregnant

person," Kari muttered. His arms were crossed over his chest, which didn't help because it drew attention to his stomach.

"Well, I doubt they've ever seen a pregnant *man*."

With the way Luther and the rest of his team had reacted to Seamus being in labor, Kaspar didn't think pregnant men were something humans could deal with. It would certainly explain why they were staring at Kari right now. They seemed to have a death wish, and Kaspar wasn't about to tell them to fuck off. Kari was more than able to do that himself.

Kaspar grinned when Julian stepped out. He and Calder were talking, and to Kaspar's surprise, Luther was right there with them. For all that Julian had lived alone for most of his life, or maybe because of it, he was a good judge of character, so Kaspar thought he was probably right when he said Luther was a decent person.

Julian beamed when he noticed Kaspar and Kari and walked toward them. "I wasn't sure I'd find everyone standing," he said when he got to them.

Kaspar barked out a laugh. "It was a close thing."

Kari was still scowling, but he gave his father a tiny smile. "They're still staring at me," he muttered.

Julian patted his shoulder. "Ignore them."

"How can I ignore them? They're staring as if I'm, I don't know, a weirdo. Do I have something on my nose?"

Luther cleared his throat. "I apologize for my team, but I'd like to explain *why* they're staring, if it's okay with you."

Kari looked like he might refuse, but instead, he nodded curtly.

Luther nodded back. "You see, in our world, in the *human* world, only women can get pregnant."

Kari cocked his head. "You don't have carriers?"

"I'm going to assume that carriers are the men who, like you, can get pregnant?"

"That's what the word means, yes."

"Then no, we don't have carriers. We have men and women, and that's it."

Kari's glare deepened. "Men and women? Are you saying I'm not a man?"

Luther seemed to realize he'd said the wrong thing. It would have been pretty hard for him not to. "I didn't mean to offend you. And no, I wasn't trying to say you're not a man. I was saying that human males don't have the ability to get pregnant. That's all. I apologize."

Kaspar fully expected Kari to hold a grudge and tell Luther to fuck off, but instead, he nodded, albeit begrudgingly. "Fine. But you need to get them to stop staring at my stomach. I'll kill them otherwise, and I'm not kidding."

Luther blinked and looked at Calder, who nodded. "He'll do it. You better be careful. They wouldn't be the first people he's killed, either. He's the reason we got the majority on the council."

Luther swallowed and gestured at his team. Thankfully, they scattered. They were still looking at Kari, but now that they were further away, it seemed to be less annoying for Kari.

"I hope the carrier thing won't be a problem?" Julian asked.

Luther shook his head. "I don't see why it should be. It's a surprise, and something we don't understand, but I'd like to learn from you."

Julian nodded. "Good, because Kari isn't the only man here who can get pregnant." He put a hand on his stomach. "I'm expecting, too, and so is my husband."

Kaspar's heart skipped a beat. He found himself beaming at Julian's words. They weren't married, and they hadn't even talked about it, but they might as well have been. Kaspar didn't need a ceremony to call Julian his husband. They were having two kids, and they would move together soon. Still, the word made his stomach churn in the best of ways.

Luther looked from Julian to Kaspar, then back to Julian. "Congratulations."

"Thank you.

"If you ever need anything, feel free to let me know. Even though I was sent here to keep an eye on you, I don't expect to have to arrest anyone or anything like that. I'm only here to observe, and I hope that we can cohabitate."

Julian smiled. "And that we can learn from each other."

"Exactly. As this situation just showed, there's a lot I can learn from you. I'm sure that I can teach you at least a few things."

"I'm sure you can." Julian took Kaspar's hand. "Now, if you'll excuse us, we were planning to go to lunch."

"Of course. I'm sorry for the delay. Thank you for seeing me this morning. I hope that now that Randy has left, everything will run more smoothly."

"I hope so too, but like I mentioned earlier, Jacqueline isn't going to stop. We have to expect her to do more, and probably soon."

Luther's expression became more serious, and he nodded. "We will, and we'll be by your side if you need us."

Kaspar couldn't say he'd expected that to happen. When he'd been told that a human team was coming to the forest, he'd thought they would try to hurt them, maybe take some of them away. He hadn't thought that the human team would try to integrate instead. Not that they could. They couldn't shift, and in a world full of shifters, it was weird. But they were trying, Luther especially, and Kaspar couldn't deny he was curious. He was also relieved that the human team wasn't the enemy Kaspar had thought they would be in the beginning.

Julian and the rest of the council already had more than enough enemies as it was. They might have the majority now, but some of the council members weren't okay with that.

Even with Jacqueline gone, it didn't mean they were harmless. But as Julian had said, eventually, Jacqueline would try to get revenge, and she was smart. She'd almost succeeded already, and only Luther's state of mind had saved them from a fight. Kaspar could too easily imagine what would have happened if things had gone the other way the day Seamus had given birth, and it was terrifying.

He tried to push the thoughts away as he, Julian, Calder, and Kari, walked toward the dining hall.

"You're thinking awfully hard," Julian teased him.

"I was just wondering what was next. I hate to think that Jacqueline is out there plotting."

Julian sighed. "Me, too, especially with the babies coming. But we don't have a choice. Until she takes the first step, we can only wait."

"I hate waiting."

"I know. But there's no way out of this. We'll keep an eye on her, and on the human team."

"You seemed to get along just fine right now," Kaspar pointed out.

"Luther isn't a bad man. I think he might be slightly too optimistic when he says that we can learn from each other, but his heart is in the right place. He said he would be there for us if we need him, and I truly believe he will. We found an ally in the most unexpected place, and we should count ourselves lucky for that."

Kaspar counted himself lucky for a lot of things—finding Julian and falling in love with him. Having Julian love him back. Getting pregnant. Building a home and a family.

Yes, he had a lot to count himself lucky for, and even though he was terrified of what the future would be like with Jacqueline waiting on the sideline, he also couldn't wait to start living.

Epilogue

Julian leaned back in his chair, smiling as he rubbed his stomach. The bump was visible now, and he expected the baby to start kicking any day. He was still hungry, but this pregnancy had brought heartburn, so he knew better than to stuff himself full.

"I'm going to explode," Kari whined. "And not because I ate too much. I want to eat more. There's just no space in my body, because this baby is taking all of it"

Julian laughed. "How long do you still have again?"

Kari glared at him. "You know how long I still have."

"The last month is always the longest one. You're ready to meet your baby, but he's not quite ready to come out. He will, though." Julian paused. "Eventually."

Kari glared at him, but he stayed in his seat. He was finding it hard to move now that he was eight months pregnant, and Julian enjoyed teasing him. As long as Kari knew that it was just teasing, things were okay.

Things were going well for them, so much better than Julian had expected. When he thought about how he'd arrived here in cete territory less than a year ago, with his son dragging him away from the only home he'd known for the past twenty-some years, and what he had now, he could hardly believe it.

He and Kaspar had moved into their new home a few weeks ago. Calum had come with them. After getting to know him, Julian had found that he quite liked him. Now that they didn't have so many people around, Calum had revealed himself to be a nice person. He was more talkative, and he didn't hide in his bedroom anymore. He still had his moments of loneliness, but Julian let him be. He had no idea what Calum's life before coming to the Bishop House had been like, and he hoped that eventually, Calum would tell him.

Julian couldn't help it. He was starting to think of Calum as another son, and he didn't mind. It might seem weird since he was pregnant, but he was forty-two after all. Well, almost forty-three by now. Calum was only twenty, younger than Kari, so he definitely could have been Julian's son, and since Julian hadn't heard anything about Calum's actual parents, he didn't mind taking on that role. He loved it, actually.

"Wait until you're as big as me," Kari said.

Julian put both his hands on his stomach. "I've already been through this. I lived to tell the tale, and so will you."

"I'm never having another baby," Kari said. He sounded convinced.

"If you don't want one, then don't have one." He might change his mind. Julian wouldn't care either way, and he knew Calder wouldn't either. Whatever Kari wanted, he would get. Calder thought Kari deserved the world, or at the very least, everything he'd always wanted.

"Where's Calum?" Calder asked.

Calum usually ate with them when they came for dinner, but not tonight. "In his bedroom. He said something about having to make a phone call and wanting to give us some family time."

Calder frowned. "Doesn't he realize he's part of the family?"

Julian shook his head. "I don't think he does. I don't know what happened to him when he was with the bats, but it doesn't seem to me like he even knows what a family's like, or that he had anything like it. It's going to take him a while to get used to it."

"Like it took a while for Kari to get used to me."

"That's only because you're a dick," Kari said. "My dad and Kaspar are angels. Calum will get used to them and me in no time."

Calder pressed a hand over his chest. "I love it when you say sweet things to me."

Kari grinned at him. "I said you're a dick. You're a lovely dick, but still a dick."

Julian relaxed. This was his life now, and he couldn't have been happier. There was still a hint of uncertainty and wariness, mostly because so far, Jacqueline hadn't done anything. No one even knew where she was. She'd left coyote territory, and after she'd talked to Randy and had convinced him to come to cete territory, no one had seen her. Julian didn't know what she was planning, but he was convinced they hadn't seen the end of her. And when she struck, things would end badly. He could only pray his family would be okay.

At least they wouldn't be alone. The council was finally working like a well-oiled machine, and to Julian's surprise, the human team had integrated well. They spent their time traveling from territory to territory, talking to people and trying to understand how the forest worked. It was more work than they'd expected. It gave them something to do, for which Julian was grateful. He might be okay with Luther, but the others still made him nervous, especially now that he was visibly pregnant. He'd caught several of them staring at him, and it made him uncomfortable. He understood they found it curious, but that didn't mean he enjoyed feeling like he was on display.

But all in all, things were peaceful. Julian knew that wouldn't last forever. He was already shielding himself for what would happen next, even though he didn't know what it was. It was hard to live that way, but he had to. He needed to focus on what he had — his family and his job. *The people he loved.* That was all he could do, and he was more than happy to do it.

He leaned against Kaspar, and Kaspar wrapped an arm around his shoulders. Julian laughed when both he and Kaspar reached for the other's stomach at the same time. He snuggled closer and rubbed Kaspar's bump, smiling at the thought that his baby was growing inside it.

"Tired?" Kaspar asked.

"I could do with a nap."

"So could I. Growing a kid is more work than I expected."

"You're doing well," Julian told him, tilting his head to kiss his jaw.

"Thank God. You're doing well, too. Not that you need me to tell you that."

"Everything will be okay, right?" Julian asked, suddenly unsure.

Kaspar couldn't know what he was talking about, and if he was honest with himself, he didn't know himself. But Kaspar nodded anyway. "Everything will be all right. Whatever happens, we'll find a way, and we'll make it through. We've made it this far, in spite of everything. Nothing can stop us now."

Excerpt

Leon rolled on his stomach and looked at Manuel. He couldn't remember the last time he'd seen his best friend behaving this way. Manuel was checking his reflection in the mirror, even though he already knew that Curtis, his boyfriend, was a sure thing. "You know he's not going to care even if your hair is not perfect," Leon pointed out.

Manuel looked at him through the mirror. "I know. I still want to the perfect for him."

Leon sighed. He wanted to look perfect for someone, too. He knew better than to expect or hope that he would ever have what Manuel had with Curtis, though. "Tell me about his family." Leon was curious, both about Curtis and his family. Curtis had six brothers, and that wasn't something Leon had experience with.

Manuel smiled. "They're all great. The younger brothers are a bit weird, but I think that's because they're not sure what to make of me. They're all single, you know? I'm the first serious relationship any of them has, or at least, the first serious relationship they know is going to last."

Leon frowned. "No offense, but how can they know you and Curtis will last?"

Manuel shrugged. "I know. I mean, I'm not going anywhere, and neither is Curtis. That has to mean something, right? I can feel it. He's the guy for me, and I'm not about to do anything that can jeopardize our future."

Leon narrowed his eyes, but even though he knew Manuel was hiding something from him, he didn't ask. When and if Manuel was ready to tell him about it, he would be there. In the meantime, he didn't mind listening to what Curtis' brothers were up to.

He couldn't help but think about Manuel going to Sunday dinner with all those guys. Of course, Manuel only had eyes for Curtis, But Leon wanted to meet the other brothers, too. Were they as hot as Curtis? There was bound to be least one or two of them who weren't, but Curtis was damn sexy, and Leon wondered if maybe one of his brothers might be the man for him.

But no. He already knew the answer to that question. Meeting them wouldn't change it.

"And they welcomed you okay?" he asked.

Manuel smiled. "Yeah. You could come along if you want? I'm sure Curtis' mother won't mind. I mean, she already has to feed eight men and herself, and you eat like a bird. It wouldn't change anything for her."

It was tempting to say yes. Leon couldn't remember the last time he'd had a home-cooked meal. He certainly wasn't one for cooking, which meant that he usually survived on sandwiches-and take out. He also wanted to spend more time with Manuel. Now that Manuel had Curtis, it felt like they didn't see each other often enough.

But he knew better than to accept the invitation. Parents didn't like him. He knew why, and he wasn't about to change, but he didn't want Manuel to be offended or disappointed. Manuel liked Curtis and his family, and from the way things were going, Leon suspected he would be part of that family for a long time. Hell, Curtis was already moving in with him, and they'd only known each other for a few months.

Things between Manuel and Curtis were serious, and while Leon was happy for his best friend, he also couldn't help but feel like he was losing him in a way. "I can't come, but if you want, I can help with the move."

Manuel snorted. "You mean that you can keep an eye on Curtis' brothers while they move his stuff?"

Leon grinned. "Of course. Isn't that what I just said?"

Manuel turned around and leaned against the dresser. "I'll be happy to have your help. Curtis doesn't have a lot of stuff, though. I doubt there will be much for you to do, considering he has six brothers. But of course, you're welcome to come."

Leon grinned and sat up, crossing his legs under himself. "I wouldn't miss it for anything. Like you said, he has six brothers. If there anything like him, I can't wait to watch them work." He wiggled his eyebrows so Manuel knew what he was talking about.

Manuel shook his head, amused. "They're all single as far as I know."

"Oh, I'm not looking for anyone to fill my bed, don't worry."

Manuel frowned, and Leon knew he shouldn't have said that. He'd been trying to hide how lonely he was from his best friend for a while, and he wasn't doing a good job, especially not since Curtis had appeared in the picture. Leon was distracted, which meant that he needed to be more careful. He didn't want Manuel to worry about him. He didn't want anyone to worry about him.

He did enough worrying on his own.

"Are you sure you don't want to come?" Manuel asked.

Leon shook his head. "I'm sure. They're your family. You should spend time with them."

"You're my family, too. You can come. I told you they wouldn't mind. If anything, they'll be happy to meet you. I might have mentioned you a few times, and Curtis knows you."

Leon shook his head and reached for his shoes on the floor. "I'll go home. I have things to do."

"Things to do? Like what?"

Leon looked at Manuel. He knew his friend didn't believe him, but that was okay. As long as Leon could continue faking, everything would be fine. "Well, I need to do my nails. I'm not crazy about this color I chose last time."

"And you can't do that another day?"

Leon huffed and crossed his arms over his chest, glaring at Manuel. "What do you want from me? I told you I don't want to come. Are Hughing to force me?"

Manuel jerked back, and Leon felt instantly guilty. He hated pushing his best friend away. He knew Manuel was badgering him only because he cared and worried. That didn't make it easier to deal with, though. Leon understood where Manuel was coming from, and he was grateful to have his best friend in his life, but right now, he wanted to be alone.

He knew that if he pushed, Manuel would eventually give up and leave him behind. That wasn't what Leon wanted, though. He loved Manuel, albeit not in the same way Curtis loved him. But Leon knew that he was weird. He knew he was defective, and he only had Manuel in his life. Maybe it would be better for everyone if Manuel stepped out of it, but Leon couldn't bring himself to push his only friend away.

He cleared his throat. "Maybe I'll go to a bar or something. I might find some company."

"Leon—"

Leon shook his head again. "No. I know you want me to be part of your family, and I'm grateful for it. I love you. You know that. But I can't have what you and Curtis have, and that's okay. I need you to stop pushing, though."

"I don't understand why you think you can't have it. I know you like using guys and throwing them away like dirty tissues, and that's fine. It's never been my thing, but I don't have anything against it if that's what you enjoy. I'm just not sure you still enjoying it."

Leon rubbed his face, careful of his eyes. He didn't want to smudge his mascara or the dark eyeliner around his eyes. "I know you don't understand, and I don't need you to. I just need to support me. Please."

"Of course I'll support you. I wish I could do more, though."

"There's nothing to do." Leon got to his feet and forced himself to smile. "I'm fine. I promise. You'll be the first one to know if that changes, but right now, you should focus on Curtis. The two of you haven't been together long, and I can't believe he's moving in with you already," Leon said.

He was slightly worried. This wasn't like Manuel, and he couldn't help but wonder if maybe losing his mom was still hitting Manuel as hard as it had in the beginning. He wanted to do something, but he knew it would be hard. Manuel hadn't lost just anyone. He'd lost his mom, and that would leave traces for a long time. Maybe finding Curtis was the best thing that could happen to him. Leon still wished things hadn't changed between them, but he understood how ridiculous that thought was.

Manuel had Curtis now. He might not want to leave Leon behind, but Leon needed to start living without Manuel at his side.

The problem was that he wasn't sure he could.

ABOUT THE AUTHOR

Catherine is the creator of several series, most of them paranormal, including the Whitedell Pride Series and the Gillham Pack Series. While she graduated in translation, she decided to go the writer's way because it was more fun to create her own stories and characters.

She's been living in Italy for more than twenty years, but she's a daughter of the North—Belgium to be precise—and she misses it so much that she's already planning to move back.

She loves pizza—probably too much—her son, her pets, and of course, books. She sneaks some reading time into her schedule every time she has five minutes free from writing, demands from her various pets and son, and lastly, housework.

Connect with her:

lievens.catherine@gmail.com

BookBub: https://www.bookbub.com/authors/catherine-lievens

Website: https://authorcatherinelievens.wordpress.com/

Facebook: https://www.facebook.com/catherine.lievens.9

Facebook Group: https://www.facebook.com/groups/411788002341528/

Twitter: https://twitter.com/authorCLievens

Newsletter: http://eepurl.com/c-uvKn